THE FOLGER LIBRARY SHAKESPEARE

Designed to make Shakespeare's classic plays available to the general reader, each edition contains a reliable text with modernized spelling and punctuation, scene-by-scene plot summaries, and explanatory notes clarifying obscure and obsolete expressions. An interpretive essay and accounts of Shakespeare's life and theater form an instructive preface to each play.

Louis B. Wright, General Editor, was the Director of the Folger Shakespeare Library from 1948 until his retirement in 1968. He is the author of *Middle-Class Culture in Elizabethan England, Religion and Empire, Shakespeare for Everyman,* and many other books and essays on the history and literature of the Tudor and Stuart periods.

Virginia Lamar, Assistant Editor, served as research assistant to the Director and Executive Secretary of the Folger Shakespeare Library from 1946 until her death in 1968. She is the author of *English Dress in the Age of Shakespeare* and *Travel and Roads in England,* and coeditor of William Strachey's *Historie of Travell into Virginia Britania.*

The Folger Shakespeare Library

The Folger Shakespeare Library in Washington, D.C., a research institute founded and endowed by Henry Clay Folger and administered by the Trustees of Amherst College, contains the world's largest collection of Shakespeareana. Although the Folger Library's primary purpose is to encourage advanced research in history and literature, it has continually exhibited a profound concern in stimulating a popular interest in the Elizabethan period.

The Folger Library General Reader's Shakespeare

The First Part
of
Henry the Sixth

by

WILLIAM
SHAKESPEARE

WASHINGTON SQUARE PRESS
PUBLISHED BY POCKET BOOKS
New York   London   Toronto   Sydney   Tokyo

Most Washington Square Press Books are available at special quantity discounts for bulk purchases for sales promotions, premiums or fund raising. Special books or book excerpts can also be created to fit specific needs.

For details write the office of the Vice President of Special Markets, Pocket Books, 1230 Avenue of the Americas, New York, New York 10020.

A Washington Square Press Publication of
POCKET BOOKS, a division of Simon & Schuster, Inc.
1230 Avenue of the Americas, New York, N.Y. 10020

ISBN: 0-671-66918-4

First Washington Square Press printing September 1966

13 12 11 10 9 8 7 6 5 4

WASHINGTON SQUARE PRESS and WSP colophon are
registered trademarks of Simon & Schuster, Inc.

Printed in the U.S.A.

Preface

This edition of *The First Part of Henry VI* is designed to make available a readable text of what is chronologically the fifth of a series of plays dealing with English history. In the centuries since Shakespeare, many changes have occurred in the meanings of words, and some clarification of Shakespeare's vocabulary may be helpful. To provide the reader with necessary notes in the most accessible format, we have placed them on the pages facing the text that they explain. We have tried to make these notes as brief and simple as possible. Preliminary to the text we have also included a brief statement of essential information about Shakespeare and his stage. Readers desiring more detailed information should refer to the books suggested in the references, and if still further information is needed, the bibliographies in those books will provide the necessary clues to the literature of the subject.

The early texts of Shakespeare's plays provide only scattered stage directions and no indications of setting, and it is conventional for modern editors to add these to clarify the action. Such additions, and additions to entrances and exits, as well as many indications of act and scene divisions, are placed in square brackets.

All illustrations are from material in the Folger Library collections.

L. B. W.
V. A. L.

February 1, 1966

Henry the fift.

THis was a King Renowned neere and far,
   A *Mars* of men, a Thunderbolt of war:
At *Agencourt* the French were ouerthrowne,
And *Henry* heyre proclaim'd vnto that Crowne.
In nine yeeres raigne this valiant Prince wan more,
Then all the Kings did after, or before.
Entomb'd at *Westminster* his Carkas lyes,
His foule did (like his Acts) ascend the skyes.

Henry the Fifth and laudatory verse. From John Taylor, *A Memorial of All the English Monarchs* (1622).

The Dangers of Civil Strife

The last third of the sixteenth century saw a new and increasing spirit of nationalism in England. This nationalistic spirit was reflected in an outpouring of lyric poetry, narrative poetry, prose chronicles, and stage plays that in some fashion dealt with England's past. Indeed, throughout the sixteenth and seventeenth centuries, historical writings of many sorts enjoyed a popularity and an acclaim equaled by few other forms of literature. The Renaissance revived an interest in Greek and Roman history, and in every country of Western Europe this interest in history in general stirred a fresh concern over that nation's own past.

History was believed to have profound truths to impart: practical, political, and moral. From examples in the past men would learn what to avoid and what to emulate. From wicked characters who came to bad ends they could perceive that the wages of sin would be trouble and disaster; and from good and noble figures they could learn the virtues to be cultivated and imitated. History, in short, presented a mirror of life useful to every individual, whether of high or low degree.

A collection of historical narratives in verse with commentaries in prose that influenced Shakespeare's age was *A Mirror for Magistrates,* first published in

1559; with successive augmentations, it remained in print until after the turn of the century. From the *Mirror for Magistrates,* Shakespeare and his contemporaries drew factual information, as well as a philosophic point of view about the deeds of English kings, both recent and mythological. In the *Mirror,* ghosts of past rulers related in verse their own stories to the authors, who appended prose commentaries pointing the moral lessons to be deduced. *A Mirror for Magistrates* was one of the important vehicles for popularizing historical knowledge about, and comment upon, England's rulers.

Prose chronicles of England enjoyed an enormous popularity in the sixteenth century. One of the most important of these chronicles for Shakespeare's purposes was Edward Hall's *The Union of the Two Noble and Illustrious Families of Lancaster and York,* first published in 1542 and reprinted four times thereafter with slightly varying title pages. Hall (sometimes spelled Halle) begins with a section on "The Unquiet Time of King Henry the Fourth" and ends with one on "The Triumphant Reign of King Henry the Eighth." He thus deals with the Wars of the Roses and brings his work to a climax with the establishment of the Tudors as firm rulers of a settled kingdom. Hall was not content merely to relate events of the past, as earlier chroniclers had done, but he made historical judgments, showed a concern with cause and effect, and provided a considerable amount of moralizing. His purpose was to glorify the Tudors and to drive home the lesson that weak rulers, dissension in the state, civil strife, and rebellion lead to anarchy and disaster. Hall carried on a propaganda favorable to the Tudors and utilized Sir Thomas More's *History of King Richard III* to continue the blackening of the character of the King whom Henry Tudor overthrew.

The work that Shakespeare and many of his fellow poets found most convenient to use as a source for history was principally compiled by Raphael Holinshed, an editor long employed by the printer Reginald Wolfe. Wolfe had projected a vast history of England, Scotland, and Ireland but died before the task was completed. Other printers, however, supported the project, and Holinshed, with the assistance of collaborators, brought together an extensive collection of material first published in two volumes in 1577 as *The Chronicles of England, Scotland, and Ireland.* A second edition, much amplified, was published in three volumes in 1587 after Holinshed's death. This second edition was the quarry from which Shakespeare dug much of his historical material.

Another work which helped to popularize history and to give Englishmen a sense of national purpose was John Foxe's *The Acts and Monuments,* commonly known as the "Book of Martyrs," first published in 1563 and many times reprinted afterward. Not only did Foxe relate the biographies of Protestant martyrs, but he emphasized the fact that England was the "elect nation" especially chosen of God to lead Christendom in its fight against superstition and error. England thus had a manifest destiny to achieve greatness, a belief to which most patriotic Elizabethans would subscribe.

Since history was both instructive and entertaining, playwrights did not overlook opportunities to dramatize incidents and episodes based upon what they took to be historical facts. Before Shakespeare came to London to seek his fortune, chronicle plays were already popular. During the Elizabethan period approximately 220 plays dealing in some fashion with British history and historical legend were written, a number of them before Shakespeare began his own dramatic career. In Shakespeare's youth a few belated morality plays added historical characters to the personified abstractions that made up their *dramatis personae*. The earliest English tragedy, *Gorbuduc* (1562), using a tale from British legend somewhat in the manner of *King Lear*, emphasized the iniquity of rebellion and dissension, much as Shakespeare was later to do. George Peele and Robert Greene, two playwrights who preceded Shakespeare, each drew upon English history and legend for dramatic materials. Two anonymous plays utilizing historical matter that Shakespeare was later to rework were *The Troublesome Reign of King John* (*ca.* 1587) and *The Famous Victories of Henry the Fifth* (*ca.* 1588). Dozens of other plays popular when Shakespeare was a beginner in London drew upon history for subject matter.

The victory over the Spanish Armada served as a stimulus to English nationalism and stirred a further interest in patriotic poetry. Recently it has become fashionable to minimize the influence of this event upon the upsurge of patriotic writing, particularly as it affected the stage, but there can be no denial that the victory gave Englishmen a quickened interest in their national past and in the political problems of their world.

From the beginning of his career, Shakespeare showed an acute awareness of what the public wanted to see in the theatre. It is not surprising, therefore, that he should have responded to the demand for dramatized history. His first endeavors in this genre were the three parts of *Henry VI.* Formerly scholars were inclined to believe that Shakespeare wrote only the Temple Garden scene and a few other portions of Part 1, and that he also had collaborators in Parts 2 and 3. The present trend of scholarly thinking is to assign most, if not all, of the three plays to Shakespeare, though the question is still a matter of controversy. At any rate, most Shakespeare scholars nowadays appear to believe that Shakespeare is the principal author of all three parts.

Some scholars, indeed, discern a great master plan of the author for all of his history plays, beginning with *King John* as a prologue and ending with *Henry VIII* as an epilogue. The other plays fall into two linked tetralogies—*Richard II, Henry IV,* Parts 1 and 2, and *Henry V* being the first, and *Henry VI,* Parts 1, 2, and 3, and *Richard III* being the second. Scholars who accept this view of a master plan profess to see in the plays a well-knit artistic unity.

Although this view of the history plays is appealing to a sense of critical neatness and order, it does not comport with common sense or with our knowledge of theatrical conditions, then or now. If Shakespeare had come up to London with a master plan for a great sequence of ten history plays, it is unlikely that he would have begun at the wrong end of the cycle. On the contrary, the probability is that he responded to a demand for plays that someone thought the public wanted. Gradually, as he continued to supply plays based on the chronicles of the Wars of the Roses, these dramas began to fall into a pattern. At last, when they were all written and performed, something approaching unity could be seen.

It is generally believed that Parts 2 and 3 of *Henry VI* were written and performed earlier than Part 1. Sir Edmund Chambers thinks Parts 2 and 3 were performed in the season of 1590–91 and Part 1 in the season of 1591–92. After the successful performance of the two last parts, the players apparently believed that an introductory play was required to top off the account of the troubled reign of Henry VI.

That Shakespeare had the principal hand in Part 1 or was the sole author is the view of modern scholars, who no longer feel embarrassed at the playwright's treatment of his subject matter. Romantic critics, who formerly tried to find the handiwork of George Peele, Robert Greene, Thomas Nash, or Christopher Marlowe in this play, were sometimes motivated by distress over the characterization of Joan of Arc and were eager to disassociate their idolized Shakespeare from such an ungentlemanly attitude. Present-day critics, however, accustomed to the debunking of heroines no less than of heroes, are ready to accept the treatment of Joan of Arc in *Henry VI* as the normal interpretation accorded a hostile figure. It would have been difficult for Shakespeare or any other playwright of his day to present Joan of Arc, an avowed enemy of England, and French at that, as a saintly heroine. The public expected a patriotic play to deal roughly with England's enemies, male or female, and not search out hidden virtues in alien foes.

After seeing all three parts of *Henry VI* acted on the stage of the Pasadena (California) Community Playhouse, Professor R. W. Chambers declared that the experience convinced him that Shakespeare "began his career with a tetralogy based on recent history, grim, archaic, crude, yet nevertheless such as, for scope, power, patriotism, and sense of doom, had probably had no parallel since Aeschylus wrote the trilogy of which the *Persians* is the surviving fragment."[1] Another scholar, Professor E. M. W. Tillyard, after seeing the plays performed at Birmingham, England, also came away confirmed in his previous opinion that all three parts are the work of a single author, William Shakespeare.

Although the three parts of *Henry VI* were not structurally satisfactory to nineteenth-century critics, their loose, episodic construction did not bother Shakespeare's audiences any more than loose-hung plays seen on the modern stage jar audiences today. Shakespeare's audience was accustomed to drum-

---

[1] Quoted by Arthur Colby Sprague, *Shakespeare's Histories: Plays for the Stage* (London, 1964), p. 114, from Chambers, *The Jacobean Shakespeare and Measure for Measure.* Annual Shakespeare Lecture of the British Academy (London, 1937), pp. 7-8.

and-trumpet drama, with a great deal of noise, action, and bloodshed. *Henry VI* supplies these elements in abundance, and the audiences accepted it all with relish. Something was happening in every scene, and no groundling was so dull to dramatic action that he did not find items to hold his interest.

1 Henry VI is part of an historical epic, based on the English chronicles. It opens with the death of Henry V, the hero-king whom Shakespeare some years later put upon the stage, and it reveals the schemes of warring nobles to advance themselves at the expense of England. Shakespeare (if we accept him as the sole author of the play) is at pains to emphasize the dangers to the realm when the ruler is weak and powerless. The young King is pictured as a sovereign with excellent intentions, eager to bring together hostile factions. But good intentions are not enough. In the hard world of practical politics, the ruler must have the moral courage, the intelligence, the sheer strength, to enforce his will. This is one of the lessons that the play is designed to teach. Another dogma that runs through *1 Henry VI*, and all the other plays in the series beginning chronologically with *Richard II* and ending with *Richard III*, is that the sin of rebellion against an anointed sovereign brings mortal disasters. The Duke of Exeter's mournful words (III, i) suggest this theme:

> This late dissension grown betwixt the peers
> Burns under feigned ashes of forged love,
> And will at last break out into a flame.
> As festered members rot but by degree,

Till bones and flesh and sinews fall away,
So will this base and envious discord breed.
And now I fear that fatal prophecy
Which in the time of Henry named the Fifth
Was in the mouth of every sucking babe:
That Henry born at Monmouth should win all
And Henry born at Windsor should lose all:
Which is so plain that Exeter doth wish
His days may finish ere that hapless time.

In *1 Henry VI* the dramatist pictures the punishment that the realm of England must endure as the result of past sins and present weakness in the state. Destiny has made France the instrument of this retribution, with Joan of Arc as the agent of France's successful action. Joan of Arc, portrayed as a witch capable of calling up the Powers of Darkness to do her bidding, stands in contrast with the nominal king of the English, pious, maundering, and ineffective.

As in verse epics, the play has a hero of supreme courage and virtue, Lord Talbot, who sacrifices his life, as his son also gives his life, for England. Thomas Nash, in *Pierce Penniless His Supplication to the Devil* (1592), commented: "How would it have joyed brave Talbot, the terror of the French, after he had lien [lain] two hundred years in his tomb, to think that he should triumph again on the stage and have his bones new embalmed with the tears of ten thousand spectators at least (at several times), who, in the tragedian that represents his person, imagine they behold him fresh bleeding!" So important are the Talbot scenes that some critics

have thought that *1 Henry VI* incorporated material
from some earlier play in which Talbot was the hero.

The political lessons implicit in *Henry VI* are
found ready-made in the chronicles, particularly in
Edward Hall's *The Union of the Two Noble and
Illustrious Families of Lancaster and York*, and in
successive editions of the *Book of Homilies*, which
has two sermons against the sin of rebellion, in *A
Mirror for Magistrates*, and in various other writings
of the time. Shakespeare was expressing ideas widely
current and sincerely held by his contemporaries.

The principal sources of *Henry VI* are to be found
in Holinshed's *Chronicles*, the most readily available
work. But the dramatist clearly drew upon Hall, and
he appears to have consulted other chroniclers as
well: Fabyan, Grafton, and Stow. Although the possibility that the three parts of *Henry VI* as they
exist were based on earlier plays cannot be ruled out
completely, recent scholarship inclines to the view
they were newly written from material taken directly
from the chronicles.

The author of *1 Henry VI* showed no compunction
about telescoping time to suit the requirements of
stage production. When the play opens at the funeral of King Henry V, his heir is an infant, but by
the beginning of Act V, Henry VI is a young man
of marriageable age. The spectator is hardly aware
of time at all but is swept along in a sequence of
rapid action that appears to be timeless. Some
episodes in the play are fictional rather than factual,
but in the minds of spectators they become part of
the accepted historical story. There is no proof of

the meeting between the factions of York and Lancaster in the Temple Garden, but Shakespeare has made it one of the most widely believed episodes in medieval English history.

The plays on Henry VI were undoubtedly popular when first performed in London, but their stage history is vague and indefinite. These loosely constructed plays soon lost their appeal and theatrical history reveals few revivals before modern times. One performance of *1 Henry VI* is recorded at Drury Lane Theatre in London in 1738. Edmund Kean in 1817 patched together a play from all three parts of *Henry VI* and produced it in London under the name of *Richard Duke of York*. In 1889 Osmond Tearle adapted *1 Henry VI* for a production at Stratford-upon-Avon. The three parts of *Henry VI* were performed at the Stratford Festival in 1906 by a company led by Sir Frank Benson. Since that time the *Henry VI* plays have been kept alive by academic groups and little theatres.

In addition, in recent years, several professional companies have staged the trilogy with extraordinary success. In 1963 the Royal Shakespeare Company made adaptations of the three parts, boiling them down into two versions entitled *Henry VI* and *Edward IV*. They followed these with Shakespeare's *Richard III*. The whole saga appeared under the general title of *The Wars of the Roses* and proved so popular that they were repeated in 1964 as part of the Shakespeare Four Hundredth Anniversary celebration at Stratford. An abbreviated version of this adaptation appeared on television in 1966, and

in the same year the Stratford Festival company of
Ontario, Canada, produced a similar adaptation of
Henry VI. No one who saw the Stratford productions in 1963 or 1964 doubted their theatrical effec-
tiveness. If audiences in the 1960's can sit spellbound
by these plays, Shakespeare's contemporaries must
have found even greater fascination in the dramatic
portrayal of events which had for them a much
greater emotional impact. Shakespeare, or whoever
strung together the episodes that make up the *Henry
VI* plays, knew what he was doing. Sir Barry Jack-
son, in an article entitled "On Producing *Henry VI*," [2]
comments: "What is as clear as daylight from the
practical view of stage production is that the author
[of the *Henry VI* plays] was a dramatist of the first
rank, though perhaps immature. If the author was
not Shakespeare, I can only regret that the writer
in question did not give us more examples of his
genius. In short, *Henry VI* is eminently actable."

THE TEXT

The text of *1 Henry VI* is based on the first
printing of the play in the Folio of 1623. No quarto
version exists. Stage directions, more numerous and
more explicit than in most of the other plays, in
some instances suggest that the printers used the
author's copy. The nature of the stage directions
indicates that the copy may have been marked for
use by the actors.

[2] *Shakespeare Survey 6* (Cambridge, 1953), p. 50.

THE AUTHOR

As early as 1598 Shakespeare was so well known as a literary and dramatic craftsman that Francis Meres, in his *Palladis Tamia: Wits Treasury*, referred in flattering terms to him as "mellifluous and honey-tongued Shakespeare," famous for his *Venus and Adonis*, his *Lucrece*, and "his sugared sonnets," which were circulating "among his private friends." Meres observes further that "as Plautus and Seneca are accounted the best for comedy and tragedy among the Latins, so Shakespeare among the English is the most excellent in both kinds for the stage," and he mentions a dozen plays that had made a name for Shakespeare. He concludes with the remark that "the Muses would speak with Shakespeare's fine filed phrase if they would speak English."

To those acquainted with the history of the Elizabethan and Jacobean periods, it is incredible that anyone should be so naïve or ignorant as to doubt the reality of Shakespeare as the author of the plays that bear his name. Yet so much nonsense has been written about other "candidates" for the plays that it is well to remind readers that no credible evidence that would stand up in a court of law has ever been adduced to prove either that Shakespeare did not write his plays or that anyone else wrote them. All the theories offered for the authorship of Francis Bacon, the Earl of Derby, the Earl of Oxford, the Earl of Hertford, Christopher Marlowe, and a score of other candidates are mere conjectures spun from the active imaginations of persons who confuse hypothesis and conjecture with evidence.

As Meres's statement of 1598 indicates, Shakespeare was already a popular playwright whose name carried weight at the box office. The obvious reputation of Shakespeare as early as 1598 makes the effort to prove him a myth one of the most absurd in the history of human perversity.

The anti-Shakespeareans talk darkly about a plot of vested interests to maintain the authorship of Shakespeare. Nobody has any vested interest in Shakespeare, but every scholar is interested in the truth and in the quality of evidence advanced by special pleaders who set forth hypotheses in place of facts.

The anti-Shakespeareans base their arguments upon a few simple premises, all of them false. These false premises are that Shakespeare was an unlettered yokel without any schooling, that nothing is known about Shakespeare, and that only a noble lord or the equivalent in background could have written the plays. The facts are that more is known about Shakespeare than about most dramatists of his day, that he had a very good education, acquired in the Stratford Grammar School, that the plays show no evidence of profound book learning, and that the knowledge of kings and courts evident in the plays is no greater than any intelligent young man could have picked up at second hand. Most anti-Shakespeareans are naïve and betray an obvious snobbery. The author of their favorite plays, they imply, must have had a college diploma framed and hung on his study wall like the one in their dentist's office, and obviously so great a writer must have had a title or some equally significant evidence of exalted social background. They forget that genius has a way of cropping up in unexpected places and that none of the great creative writers of the world got his inspiration in a college or university course.

William Shakespeare was the son of John Shakespeare of Stratford-upon-Avon, a substantial citizen of that small but busy market town in the center of the rich agricultural county of Warwick. John Shakespeare kept a shop, what we would call a general store; he dealt in wool and other produce and gradually acquired property. As a youth, John Shakespeare had learned the trade of glover and leather worker. There is no contemporary evidence that the elder Shakespeare was a butcher, though the anti-Shakespeareans like to talk about the ignorant "butcher's boy of Stratford." Their only evidence is a statement by gossipy John Aubrey, more than a century after William Shakespeare's birth, that young William followed his father's trade, and when he killed a calf, "he would do it in a high style and make a speech." We would like to believe the story true, but Aubrey is not a very credible witness.

John Shakespeare probably continued to operate a farm at Snitterfield that his father had leased. He married Mary Arden, daughter of his father's land-

lord, a man of some property. The third of their
eight children was William, baptized on April 26,
1564, and probably born three days before. At least,
it is conventional to celebrate April 23 as his birth-
day.

The Stratford records give considerable information about John Shakespeare. We know that he held
several municipal offices including those of alderman and mayor. In 1580 he was in some sort of
legal difficulty and was fined for neglecting a sum-
mons of the Court of Queen's Bench requiring him
to appear at Westminster and be bound over to
keep the peace.

As a citizen and alderman of Stratford, John
Shakespeare was entitled to send his son to the
grammar school free. Though the records are lost,
there can be no reason to doubt that this is where
young William received his education. As any student of the period knows, the grammar schools provided the basic education in Latin learning and literature. The Elizabethan grammar school is not to
be confused with modern grammar schools. Many
cultivated men of the day received all their formal
education in the grammar schools. At the universities in this period a student would have received
little training that would have inspired him to be a
creative writer. At Stratford young Shakespeare
would have acquired a familiarity with Latin and
some little knowledge of Greek. He would have
read Latin authors and become acquainted with
the plays of Plautus and Terence. Undoubtedly, in
this period of his life he received that stimulation

to read and explore for himself the world of ancient and modern history which he later utilized in his plays. The youngster who does not acquire this type of intellectual curiosity *before* college days rarely develops as a result of a college course the kind of mind Shakespeare demonstrated. His learning in books was anything but profound, but he clearly had the probing curiosity that sent him in search of information, and he had a keenness in the observation of nature and of humankind that finds reflection in his poetry.

There is little documentation for Shakespeare's boyhood. There is little reason why there should be. Nobody knew that he was going to be a dramatist about whom any scrap of information would be prized in the centuries to come. He was merely an active and vigorous youth of Stratford, perhaps assisting his father in his business, and no Boswell bothered to write down facts about him. The most important record that we have is a marriage license issued by the Bishop of Worcester on November 27, 1582, to permit William Shakespeare to marry Anne Hathaway, seven or eight years his senior; furthermore, the Bishop permitted the marriage after reading the banns only once instead of three times, evidence of the desire for haste. The need was explained on May 26, 1583, when the christening of Susanna, daughter of William and Anne Shakespeare, was recorded at Stratford. Two years later, on February 2, 1585, the records show the birth of twins to the Shakespeares, a boy and a girl who were christened Hamnet and Judith.

What William Shakespeare was doing in Stratford during the early years of his married life, or when he went to London, we do not know. It has been conjectured that he tried his hand at schoolteaching, but that is a mere guess. There is a legend that he left Stratford to escape a charge of poaching in the park of Sir Thomas Lucy of Charlecote, but there is no proof of this. There is also a legend that when first he came to London he earned his living by holding horses outside a playhouse and presently was given employment inside, but there is nothing better than eighteenth-century hearsay for this. How Shakespeare broke into the London theatres as a dramatist and actor we do not know. But lack of information is not surprising, for Elizabethans did not write their autobiographies, and we know even less about the lives of many writers and some men of affairs than we know about Shakespeare. By 1592 he was so well established and popular that he incurred the envy of the dramatist and pamphleteer Robert Greene, who referred to him as an "upstart crow . . . in his own conceit the only Shake-scene in a country." From this time onward, contemporary allusions and references in legal documents enable the scholar to chart Shakespeare's career with greater accuracy than is possible with most other Elizabethan dramatists.

By 1594 Shakespeare was a member of the company of actors known as the Lord Chamberlain's Men. After the accession of James I, in 1603, the company would have the sovereign for their patron

and would be known as the King's Men. During the
period of its greatest prosperity, this company
would have as its principal theatres the Globe and
the Blackfriars. Shakespeare was both an actor and
a shareholder in the company. Tradition has assigned him such acting roles as Adam in *As You
Like It* and the Ghost in *Hamlet,* a modest place
on the stage that suggests that he may have had
other duties in the management of the company.
Such conclusions, however, are based on surmise.

What we do know is that his plays were popular
and that he was highly successful in his vocation.
His first play may have been *The Comedy of Er-
rors,* acted perhaps in 1591. Certainly this was one
of his earliest plays. The three parts of *Henry VI*
were acted sometime between 1590 and 1592.
Critics are not in agreement about precisely how
much Shakespeare wrote of these three plays.
Richard III probably dates from 1593. With this
play Shakespeare captured the imagination of Elizabethan audiences, then enormously interested in
historical plays. With *Richard III* Shakespeare also
gave an interpretation pleasing to the Tudors of the
rise to power of the grandfather of Queen Elizabeth.
From this time onward, Shakespeare's plays followed
on the stage in rapid succession: *Titus Andronicus,
The Taming of the Shrew, The Two Gentlemen of
Verona, Love's Labor's Lost, Romeo and Juliet,
Richard II, A Midsummer Night's Dream, King
John, The Merchant of Venice, Henry IV (Parts 1
and 2), Much Ado about Nothing, Henry V, Julius
Caesar, As You Like It, Twelfth Night, Hamlet, The*

*Merry Wives of Windsor, All's Well That Ends
Well, Measure for Measure, Othello, King Lear,* and
nine others that followed before Shakespeare retired
completely, about 1613.

In the course of his career in London, he made
enough money to enable him to retire to Stratford
with a competence. His purchase on May 4, 1597,
of New Place, then the second-largest dwelling in
Stratford, "a pretty house of brick and timber," with
a handsome garden, indicates his increasing prosperity. There his wife and children lived while he
busied himself in the London theatres. The summer before he acquired New Place, his life was
darkened by the death of his only son, Hamnet, a
child of eleven. In May, 1602, Shakespeare pur-
chased one hundred and seven acres of fertile farm-
land near Stratford and a few months later bought
a cottage and garden across the alley from New
Place. About 1611, he seems to have returned per-
manently to Stratford, for the next year a legal docu-
ment refers to him as "William Shakespeare of
Stratford-upon-Avon . . . gentleman." To achieve
the desired appellation of gentleman, William
Shakespeare had seen to it that the College of Heralds in 1596 granted his father a coat of arms. In
one step he thus became a second-generation gentleman.

Shakespeare's daughter Susanna made a good
match in 1607 with Dr. John Hall, a prominent and
prosperous Stratford physician. His second daughter, Judith, did not marry until she was thirty-one
years old, and then, under somewhat scandalous cir-

cumstances, she married Thomas Quiney, a Stratford vintner. On March 25, 1616, Shakespeare made his will, bequeathing his landed property to Susanna, £300 to Judith, certain sums to other relatives, and his second-best bed to his wife, Anne. Much has been made of the second-best bed, but the legacy probably indicates only that Anne liked that particular bed. Shakespeare, following the practice of the time, may have already arranged with Susanna for his wife's care. Finally, on April 23, 1616, the anniversary of his birth, William Shakespeare died, and he was buried on April 25 within the chancel of Trinity Church, as befitted an honored citizen. On August 6, 1623, a few months before the publication of the collected edition of Shakespeare's plays, Anne Shakespeare joined her husband in death.

THE PUBLICATION OF HIS PLAYS

During his lifetime Shakespeare made no effort to publish any of his plays, though eighteen appeared in print in single-play editions known as quartos. Some of these are corrupt versions known as "bad quartos." No quarto, so far as is known, had the author's approval. Plays were not considered "literature" any more than most radio and television scripts today are considered literature. Dramatists sold their plays outright to the theatrical companies and it was usually considered in the company's interest to keep plays from getting into print. To achieve a reputation as a man of letters, Shakespeare wrote his *Sonnets* and his narrative poems,

Venus and Adonis and *The Rape of Lucrece*, but he probably never dreamed that his plays would establish his reputation as a literary genius. Only Ben Jonson, a man known for his colossal conceit, had the crust to call his plays *Works*, as he did when he published an edition in 1616. But men laughed at Ben Jonson.

After Shakespeare's death, two of his old colleagues in the King's Men, John Heminges and Henry Condell, decided that it would be a good thing to print, in more accurate versions than were then available, the plays already published and eighteen additional plays not previously published in quarto. In 1623 appeared *Mr. William Shakespeares Comedies, Histories & Tragedies. Published according to the True Originall Copies. London. Printed by Isaac Iaggard and Ed. Blount.* This was the famous First Folio, a work that had the authority of Shakespeare's associates. The only play commonly attributed to Shakespeare that was omitted in the First Folio was *Pericles*. In their preface, "To the great Variety of Readers," Heminges and Condell state that whereas "you were abused with diverse stolen and surreptitious copies, maimed and deformed by the frauds and stealths of injurious impostors that exposed them, even those are now offered to your view cured and perfect of their limbs; and all the rest, absolute in their numbers, as he conceived them." What they used for printer's copy is one of the vexed problems of scholarship, and skilled bibliographers have devoted years of study to the question of the relation of the "copy" for the First Folio to Shakespeare's manuscripts. In some cases it is clear that the editors corrected printed quarto versions of the plays, probably by comparison with playhouse scripts. Whether these scripts were in Shakespeare's autograph is anybody's guess. No manuscript of any play in Shakespeare's handwriting has survived. Indeed, very few play manuscripts from this period by any author are extant. The Tudor and Stuart periods had not yet learned to prize autographs and authors' original manuscripts.

Since the First Folio contains eighteen plays not previously printed, it is the only source for these. For the other eighteen, which had appeared in quarto versions, the First Folio also has the authority of an edition prepared and overseen by Shakespeare's colleagues and professional associates. But since editorial standards in 1623 were far from strict, and Heminges and Condell were actors rather than editors by profession, the texts are sometimes careless. The printing and proofreading of the First Folio also left much to be desired, and some garbled passages have had to be corrected and emended. The "good quarto" texts have to be taken into account in preparing a modern edition.

Because of the great popularity of Shakespeare through the centuries, the First Folio has become a prized book, but it is not a very rare one, for it is estimated that 238 copies are extant. The Folger Shakespeare Library in Washington, D.C., has seventy-nine copies of the First Folio, collected by the founder, Henry Clay Folger, who believed that a collation of as many texts as possible would reveal significant facts about the text of Shakespeare's plays. Dr. Charlton Hinman, using an ingenious machine of his own invention for mechanical collating, has made many discoveries that throw light on Shakespeare's text and on printing practices of the day.

The probability is that the First Folio of 1623 had an edition of between 1,000 and 1,250 copies. It is believed that it sold for £1, which made it an expensive book, for £1 in 1623 was equivalent to something between $40 and $50 in modern purchasing power.

During the seventeenth century, Shakespeare was sufficiently popular to warrant three later editions in folio size, the Second Folio of 1632, the Third Folio of 1663–1664, and the Fourth Folio of 1685. The Third Folio added six other plays ascribed to Shakespeare, but these are apocryphal.

THE SHAKESPEAREAN THEATRE

The theatres in which Shakespeare's plays were performed were vastly different from those we know today. The stage was a platform that jutted out into the area now occupied by the first rows of seats on the main floor, what is called the "orchestra" in America and the "pit" in England. This platform had no curtain to come down at the ends of acts and scenes. And although simple stage properties were available, the Elizabethan theatre lacked both the machinery and the elaborate movable scenery of the modern theatre. In the rear of the platform stage was a curtained area that could be used as an inner room, a tomb, or any such scene that might be required. A balcony above this inner room, and perhaps balconies on the sides of the stage, could represent the upper deck of a ship, the entry to Juliet's room, or a prison window. A trap door in the stage provided an entrance for ghosts and devils from the nether regions, and a similar trap in the canopied structure over the stage, known as the "heavens," made it possible to let down angels on a rope. These primitive stage arrangements help to account for many elements in Elizabethan plays. For example, since there was no curtain, the dramatist frequently felt the necessity of writing into his play action to clear the stage at the ends of acts and scenes. The funeral march at the end of *Hamlet* is not there merely for atmosphere; Shakespeare had to get the corpses off the stage. The lack of scenery also freed the dramatist from undue concern about the exact location of his sets, and the physical relation of his various settings to each other did not have to be worked out with the same precision as in the modern theatre.

Before London had buildings designed exclusively for theatrical entertainment, plays were given in inns and taverns. The characteristic inn of the period had an inner courtyard with rooms opening onto balconies overlooking the yard. Players could set up their temporary stages at one end of the yard and audiences could find seats on the balconies out of the weather. The poorer sort could stand or sit on the cobblestones in the yard, which was open to the sky. The first theatres followed this construction, and throughout the Elizabethan period the large public theatres had a yard in front of the stage open to the weather, with two or three tiers of covered balconies extending around the theatre. This physical structure again influenced the writing of plays. Because a dramatist wanted the actors to be heard, he frequently wrote into his play orations that could be delivered with declamatory effect. He also provided spectacle, buffoonery, and broad jests to keep the riotous groundlings in the yard entertained and quiet.

In another respect the Elizabethan theatre differed greatly from ours. It had no actresses. All women's roles were taken by boys, sometimes recruited from the boys' choirs of the London churches. Some of these youths acted their roles with great skill and the Elizabethans did not seem to be aware of any incongruity. The first actresses on the professional English stage appeared after the Restoration of Charles II, in 1660, when exiled Englishmen brought back from France practices of the French stage.

London in the Elizabethan period, as now, was the center of theatrical interest, though wandering actors from time to time traveled through the country performing in inns, halls, and the houses of the nobility. The first professional playhouse, called simply The Theatre, was erected by James Burbage, father of Shakespeare's colleague Richard Burbage, in 1576 on lands of the old Holywell Priory adjacent to Finsbury Fields, a playground and park area just north of the city walls. It had the advantage of being outside the city's jurisdiction and yet was near enough to be easily accessible. Soon after The Theatre was opened, another playhouse called The Curtain was erected in the same neighborhood. Both of these playhouses had open courtyards and were probably polygonal in shape.

About the time The Curtain opened, Richard Farrant, Master of the Children of the Chapel Royal at Windsor and of St. Paul's, conceived the idea of opening a "private" theatre in the old monastery buildings of the Blackfriars, not far from St. Paul's Cathedral in the heart of the city. This theatre was ostensibly to train the choirboys in plays for presentation at Court, but Farrant managed to present plays to paying audiences and achieved considerable success until aristocratic neighbors complained and had the theatre closed. This first Blackfriars Theatre was significant, however, because it popularized the boy actors in a professional way and it paved the way for a second theatre in the Blackfriars, which Shakespeare's company took over more than thirty years later. By the last years of the sixteenth century, London had at least six professional theatres and still others were erected during the reign of James I.

The Globe Theatre, the playhouse that most people connect with Shakespeare, was erected early in 1599 on the Bankside, the area across the Thames from the city. Its construction had a dramatic beginning, for on the night of December 28, 1598,

James Burbage's sons, Cuthbert and Richard, gathered together a crew who tore down the old theatre in Holywell and carted the timbers across the river to a site that they had chosen for a new playhouse. The reason for this clandestine operation was a row with the landowner over the lease to the Holywell property. The site chosen for the Globe was another playground outside of the city's jurisdiction, a region of somewhat unsavory character. Not far away was the Bear Garden, an amphitheatre devoted to the baiting of bears and bulls. This was also the region occupied by many houses of ill fame licensed by the Bishop of Winchester and the source of substantial revenue to him. But it was easily accessible either from London Bridge or by means of the cheap boats operated by the London watermen, and it had the great advantage of being beyond the authority of the Puritanical aldermen of London, who frowned on plays because they lured apprentices from work, filled their heads with improper ideas, and generally exerted a bad influence. The aldermen also complained that the crowds drawn together in the theatre helped to spread the plague.

The Globe was the handsomest theatre up to its time. It was a large building, apparently octagonal in shape, and open like its predecessors to the sky in the center, but capable of seating a large audience in its covered balconies. To erect and operate the Globe, the Burbages organized a syndicate composed of the leading members of the dramatic company, of which Shakespeare was a member. Since it was open to the weather and depended on natural light, plays had to be given in the afternoon. This caused no hardship in the long afternoons of an English summer, but in the winter the weather was a great handicap and discouraged all except the hardiest. For that reason, in 1608 Shakespeare's company was glad to take over the lease of the second Blackfriars Theatre, a substantial, roomy hall reconstructed within the framework of the old monastery building. This theatre was protected from the weather and its stage was artificially lighted by chandeliers of candles. This became the winter playhouse for Shakespeare's company and at once proved so popular that the congestion of traffic created an embarrassing problem. Stringent regulations had to be made for the movement of coaches in the vicinity. Shakespeare's company continued to use the Globe during the summer months. In 1613 a squib fired from a cannon during a performance of *Henry VIII* fell on the thatched roof and the Globe burned to the ground. The next year it was rebuilt.

London had other famous theatres. The Rose, just west of the Globe, was built by Philip Henslowe, a semiliterate denizen of the Bankside, who became one of the most important theatrical owners and producers of the Tudor and Stuart periods. What is more important for historians, he kept a detailed account book, which provides much of our information about theatrical history in his time. Another famous theatre on the Bankside was the Swan, which a Dutch priest, Johannes de Witt, visited in 1596. The crude drawing of the stage which he made was copied by his friend Arend van Buchell;

it is one of the important pieces of contemporary evidence for theatrical construction. Among the other theatres, the Fortune, north of the city, on Golding Lane, and the Red Bull, even farther away from the city, off St. John's Street, were the most popular. The Red Bull, much frequented by apprentices, favored sensational and sometimes rowdy plays.

The actors who kept all of these theatres going were organized into companies under the protection of some noble patron. Traditionally actors had enjoyed a low reputation. In some of the ordinances they were classed as vagrants; in the phraseology of the time, "rogues, vagabonds, sturdy beggars, and common players" were all listed together as undesirables. To escape penalties often meted out to these characters, organized groups of actors managed to gain the protection of various personages of high degree. In the later years of Elizabeth's reign, a group flourished under the name of the Queen's Men; another group had the protection of the Lord Admiral and were known as the Lord Admiral's Men. Edward Alleyn, son-in-law of Philip Henslowe, was the leading spirit in the Lord Admiral's Men. Besides the adult companies, troupes of boy actors from time to time also enjoyed considerable popularity. Among these were the Children of Paul's and the Children of the Chapel Royal.

The company with which Shakespeare had a long association had for its first patron Henry Carey, Lord Hunsdon, the Lord Chamberlain, and hence they were known as the Lord Chamberlain's Men.

After the accession of James I, they became the King's Men. This company was the great rival of the Lord Admiral's Men, managed by Henslowe and Alleyn.

All was not easy for the players in Shakespeare's time, for the aldermen of London were always eager for an excuse to close up the Blackfriars and any other theatres in their jurisdiction. The theatres outside the jurisdiction of London were not immune from interference, for they might be shut up by order of the Privy Council for meddling in politics or for various other offenses, or they might be closed in time of plague lest they spread infection. During plague times, the actors usually went on tour and played the provinces wherever they could find an audience. Particularly frightening were the plagues of 1592–1594 and 1613 when the theatres closed and the players, like many other Londoners, had to take to the country.

Though players had a low social status, they enjoyed great popularity, and one of the favorite forms of entertainment at Court was the performance of plays. To be commanded to perform at Court conferred great prestige upon a company of players, and printers frequently noted that fact when they published plays. Several of Shakespeare's plays were performed before the sovereign, and Shakespeare himself undoubtedly acted in some of these plays.

REFERENCES FOR FURTHER READING

Many readers will want suggestions for further reading about Shakespeare and his times. A few references will serve as guides to further study in the
enormous literature on the subject. A simple and
useful little book is Gerald Sanders, *A Shakespeare
Primer* (New York, 1950). *A Companion to Shakespeare Studies*, edited by Harley Granville-Barker
and G. B. Harrison (Cambridge, 1934), is a valuable
guide. The most recent concise handbook of facts
about Shakespeare is Gerald E. Bentley, *Shakespeare: A Biographical Handbook* (New Haven,
1961). More detailed but not so voluminous as to
be confusing is Hazelton Spencer, *The Art and Life
of William Shakespeare* (New York, 1940), which,
like Sanders' and Bentley's handbooks, contains a
brief annotated list of useful books on various aspects of the subject. The most detailed and scholarly
work providing complete factual information about
Shakespeare is Sir Edmund Chambers, *William
Shakespeare: A Study of Facts and Problems* (2 vols.,
Oxford, 1930).

Among other biographies of Shakespeare, Joseph
Quincy Adams, *A Life of William Shakespeare*
(Boston, 1923) is still an excellent assessment of the
essential facts and the traditional information, and
Marchette Chute, *Shakespeare of London* (New
York, 1949; paperback, 1957) stresses Shakespeare's
life in the theatre. Two new biographies of Shake-
speare have recently appeared. A. L. Rowse, *William*

Shakespeare: A Biography (London, 1963; New York, 1964) provides an appraisal by a distinguished English historian, who dismisses the notion that somebody else wrote Shakespeare's plays as arrant nonsense that runs counter to known historical fact. Peter Quennell, *Shakespeare: A Biography* (Cleveland and New York, 1963) is a sensitive and intelligent survey of what is known and surmised of Shakespeare's life. Louis B. Wright, *Shakespeare for Everyman* (paperback; New York, 1964) discusses the basis of Shakespeare's enduring popularity.

The Shakespeare Quarterly, published by the Shakespeare Association of America under the editorship of James G. McManaway, is recommended for those who wish to keep up with current Shakespearean scholarship and stage productions. The *Quarterly* includes an annual bibliography of Shakespeare editions and works on Shakespeare published during the previous year.

The question of the authenticity of Shakespeare's plays arouses perennial attention. The theory of hidden cryptograms in the plays is demolished by William F. and Elizebeth S. Friedman, *The Shakespearean Ciphers Examined* (New York, 1957). A succinct account of the various absurdities advanced to suggest the authorship of a multitude of candidates other than Shakespeare will be found in R. C. Churchill, *Shakespeare and His Betters* (Bloomington, Ind., 1959). Another recent discussion of the subject, *The Authorship of Shakespeare*, by James G. McManaway (Washington, D.C., 1962), presents the evidence from contemporary records to prove

the identity of Shakespeare the actor-playwright
with Shakespeare of Stratford.

Scholars are not in agreement about the details
of playhouse construction in the Elizabethan period.
John C. Adams presents a plausible reconstruction
of the Globe in *The Globe Playhouse: Its Design and
Equipment* (Cambridge, Mass., 1942; 2nd rev. ed.,
1961). A description with excellent drawings based
on Dr. Adams' model is Irwin Smith, *Shakespeare's
Globe Playhouse: A Modern Reconstruction in Text
and Scale Drawings* (New York, 1956). Other sensible discussions are C. Walter Hodges, *The Globe
Restored* (London, 1953) and A. M. Nagler, *Shakespeare's Stage* (New Haven, 1958). Bernard Becker-
man, *Shakespeare at the Globe, 1599–1609* (New
Haven, 1962; paperback, 1962) discusses Elizabethan staging and acting techniques.

A sound and readable history of the early theatres
is Joseph Quincy Adams, *Shakespearean Playhouses:
A History of English Theatres from the Beginnings
to the Restoration* (Boston, 1917). For detailed,
factual information about the Elizabethan and
seventeenth-century stages, the definitive reference
works are Sir Edmund Chambers, *The Elizabethan
Stage* (4 vols., Oxford, 1923) and Gerald E. Bentley,
The Jacobean and Caroline Stages (5 vols., Oxford,
1941–1956).

Further information on the history of the theatre
and related topics will be found in the following
titles: T. W. Baldwin, *The Organization and Per-
sonnel of the Shakespearean Company* (Princeton,
1927); Lily Bess Campbell, *Scenes and Machines*

on the English Stage during the Renaissance (Cambridge, 1923); Esther Cloudman Dunn, *Shakespeare in America* (New York, 1939); George C. D. Odell, *Shakespeare from Betterton to Irving* (2 vols., London, 1931); Arthur Colby Sprague, *Shakespeare and the Actors: The Stage Business in His Plays (1660–1905)* (Cambridge, Mass., 1944) and *Shakespearian Players and Performances* (Cambridge, Mass., 1953); Leslie Hotson, *The Commonwealth and Restoration Stage* (Cambridge, Mass., 1928); Alwin Thaler, *Shakspere to Sheridan: A Book about the Theatre of Yesterday and To-day* (Cambridge, Mass., 1922); George C. Branam, *Eighteenth-Century Adaptations of Shakespeare's Tragedies* (Berkeley, 1956); C. Beecher Hogan, *Shakespeare in the Theatre, 1701–1800* (Oxford, 1957); Ernest Bradlee Watson, *Sheridan to Robertson: A Study of the 19th-Century London Stage* (Cambridge, Mass., 1926); and Enid Welsford, *The Court Masque* (Cambridge, Mass., 1927).

A brief account of the growth of Shakespeare's reputation is F. E. Halliday, *The Cult of Shakespeare* (London, 1947). A more detailed discussion is given in Augustus Ralli, *A History of Shakespearian Criticism* (2 vols., Oxford, 1932; New York, 1958). Harley Granville-Barker, *Prefaces to Shakespeare* (5 vols., London, 1927–1948; 2 vols., London, 1958) provides stimulating critical discussion of the plays. An older classic of criticism is Andrew C. Bradley, *Shakespearean Tragedy: Lectures on Hamlet, Othello, King Lear, Macbeth* (London, 1904; paperback, 1955). Sir Edmund Chambers, *Shake-*

speare: A Survey (London, 1935; paperback, 1958) contains short, sensible essays on thirty-four of the plays, originally written as introductions to single-play editions. Alfred Harbage, *William Shakespeare: A Reader's Guide* (New York, 1963) is a handbook to the reading and appreciation of the plays, with scene synopses and interpretation.

For the history plays see Lily Bess Campbell, *Shakespeare's "Histories": Mirrors of Elizabethan Policy* (Cambridge, 1947); John Palmer, *Political Characters of Shakespeare* (London, 1945; 1961); E. M. W. Tillyard, *Shakespeare's History Plays* (London, 1948); Irving Ribner, *The English History Play in the Age of Shakespeare* (Princeton, 1947); Max M. Reese, *The Cease of Majesty* (London, 1961); and Arthur Colby Sprague, *Shakespeare's Histories: Plays for the Stage* (London, 1964). Harold Jenkins, "Shakespeare's History Plays: 1900–1951," *Shakespeare Survey 6* (Cambridge, 1953), 1-15, provides an excellent survey of recent critical opinion on the subject.

In addition to the titles listed above, a number of other works provide critical and historical background for study of the *Henry VI* plays. Paul M. Kendall, *The Yorkist Age: Daily Life during the Wars of the Roses* (New York, 1962) devotes a chapter to a lucid summary of the course of the conflict between York and Lancaster and describes the various battles. S. B. Chrimes, *Lancastrians, Yorkists, and Henry VII* (London and New York, 1964) presents a full explication of the dynastic problem resulting from Edward III's many children and the course of events leading up to Henry VII's assumption of the throne. C. L. Kingsford, *Prejudice and Promise in Fifteenth Century England* (Oxford, 1925) has a valuable chapter on Shakespeare's treatment of fifteenth-century English history. Hereward T. Price, *Construction in Shakespeare,* University of Michigan Contributions in Modern Philology, No. 17 (Ann Arbor, 1951) argues for a unified pattern to the three parts of *Henry VI* and Shakespeare's sole authorship and defends the skill of their construction. The most recent edition of the trilogy has been edited by Andrew S. Cairncross for the new Arden series (3 vols., London and Cambridge, Mass., 1962–1964).

The comedies are illuminated by the following studies: C. L. Barber, *Shakespeare's Festive Comedy* (Princeton, 1959); John Russell Brown, *Shakespeare and His Comedies* (London, 1957); H. B. Charlton, *Shakespearian Comedy* (London, 1938; 4th ed., 1949); W. W. Lawrence, *Shakespeare's Problem Comedies* (New York, 1931); and Thomas M. Parrott, *Shakespearean Comedy* (New York, 1949).

Further discussions of Shakespeare's tragedies, in addition to Bradley, already cited, are contained in H. B. Charlton, *Shakespearian Tragedy* (Cambridge, 1948); Willard Farnham, *The Medieval Heritage of Elizabethan Tragedy* (Berkeley, 1936) and *Shakespeare's Tragic Frontier: The World of His Final Tragedies* (Berkeley, 1950); and Harold S. Wilson, *On the Design of Shakespearian Tragedy* (Toronto, 1957).

The "Roman" plays are treated in M. M. MacCallum, *Shakespeare's Roman Plays and Their Background* (London, 1910) and J. C. Maxwell, "Shakespeare's Roman Plays, 1900–1956," *Shakespeare Survey 10* (Cambridge, 1957), 1-11.

Kenneth Muir, *Shakespeare's Sources: Comedies and Tragedies* (London, 1957) discusses Shakespeare's use of source material. The sources themselves have been reprinted several times. Among old editions are John P. Collier (ed.), *Shakespeare's Library* (2 vols., London, 1850), Israel C. Gollancz (ed.), *The Shakespeare Classics* (12 vols., London, 1907–1926), and W. C. Hazlitt (ed.), *Shakespeare's Library* (6 vols., London, 1875). A modern edition is being prepared by Geoffrey Bullough with the title *Narrative and Dramatic Sources of Shakespeare* (London and New York, 1957–). Five volumes, covering the sources for the comedies, histories, and Roman plays, have been published to date (1966).

In addition to the second edition of *Webster's New International Dictionary*, which contains most of the unusual words used by Shakespeare, the following reference works are helpful: Edwin A. Abbott, *A Shakespearian Grammar* (London, 1872); C. T. Onions, *A Shakespeare Glossary* (2nd rev. ed., Oxford, 1925); and Eric Partridge, *Shakespeare's Bawdy* (New York, 1948; paperback, 1960).

Some knowledge of the social background of the period in which Shakespeare lived is important for a full understanding of his work. A brief, clear, and accurate account of Tudor history is S. T. Bindoff, *The Tudors*, in the Penguin series. A readable general history is G. M. Trevelyan, *The History of Eng-*

land, first published in 1926 and available in numerous editions. The same author's *English Social History,* first published in 1942 and also available in many editions, provides fascinating information about England in all periods. Sir John Neale, *Queen Elizabeth* (London, 1935; paperback, 1957) is the best study of the great Queen. Various aspects of life in the Elizabethan period are treated in Louis B. Wright, *Middle-Class Culture in Elizabethan England* (Chapel Hill, N.C., 1935; reprinted Ithaca, N.Y., 1958, 1964). *Shakespeare's England: An Account of the Life and Manners of His Age,* edited by Sidney Lee and C. T. Onions (2 vols., Oxford, 1917), provides much information on many aspects of Elizabethan life. A fascinating survey of the period will be found in Muriel St. C. Byrne, *Elizabethan Life in Town and Country* (London, 1925; rev. ed., 1954; paperback, 1961).

The Folger Library is issuing a series of illustrated booklets entitled "Folger Booklets on Tudor and Stuart Civilization," printed and distributed by Cornell University Press. Published to date are the following titles:

D.W. Davies, *Dutch Influences on English Culture, 1558–1625*

Giles E. Dawson, *The Life of William Shakespeare*

Ellen C. Eyler, *Early English Gardens and Garden Books*

Elaine W. Fowler, *English Sea Power in the Early Tudor Period, 1485–1558*

John R. Hale, *The Art of War and Renaissance England*

William Haller, *Elizabeth I and the Puritans*

Virginia A. LaMar, *English Dress in the Age of Shakespeare*

——, *Travel and Roads in England*

John L. Lievsay, *The Elizabethan Image of Italy*

James G. McManaway, *The Authorship of Shakespeare*

Dorothy E. Mason, *Music in Elizabethan England*

Garrett Mattingly, *The "Invincible" Armada and Elizabethan England*

Boies Penrose, *Tudor and Early Stuart Voyaging*

Conyers Read, *The Government of England under Elizabeth*

T. I. Rae, *Scotland in the Time of Shakespeare*

Albert J. Schmidt, *The Yeoman in Tudor and Stuart England*

Lilly C. Stone, *English Sports and Recreations*

Craig R. Thompson, *The Bible in English, 1525–1611*

——, *The English Church in the Sixteenth Century*

——, *Schools in Tudor England*

——, *Universities in Tudor England*

Louis B. Wright, *Shakespeare's Theatre and the Dramatic Tradition*

At intervals the Folger Library plans to gather these booklets in hardbound volumes. The first is *Life and Letters in Tudor and Stuart England, First Folger Series,* edited by Louis B. Wright and Virginia A. LaMar (published for the Folger Shakespeare Library by Cornell University Press, 1962). The volume contains eleven of the separate booklets.

From Brute to King Iames.

Henry the sixt.

THis Infant Prince scarce being nine months old,
   The Realms of *France* & *England* he did hold:
But he vncapable, throught want of yeeres,
Was ouergouern'd, by misgouern'd Peeres.
Now *Yorke* and *Lancaster*, with bloudy wars
Both wound this kingdom, with deep deadly scars
Whilst this good King by *Yorke* oppos'd; depos'd,
Expos'd to dangers is Captiu'd, inclos'd,
His Queene exilde, his Son, and many friends,
Fled, murdred, slaughter'd; lastly fate contends,
To Crowne him once againe, who then at last
VVas murdered, thirty nine yeeres being past.

Anno Dom. 1460

Henry VI and biographical verse. From John Taylor, *A Memorial of All the English Monarchs* (1662).

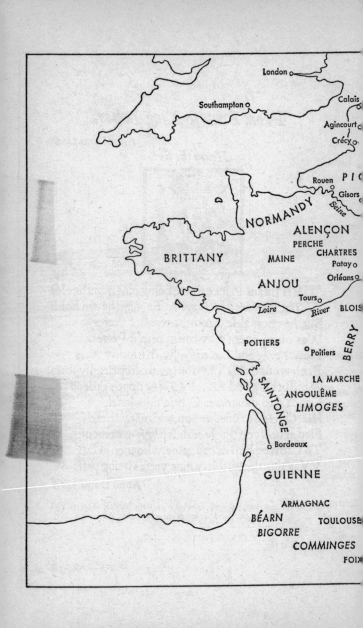

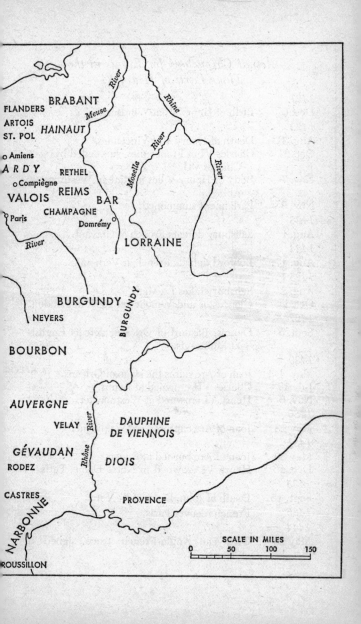

FLANDERS
ARTOIS
ST. POL

BRABANT

HAINAUT

Meuse River

Rhine River

Moselle River

River

o Amiens

ARDY

RETHEL

o Compiègne

VALOIS

REIMS

BAR

o Paris

CHAMPAGNE

Domrémy o

River

LORRAINE

BURGUNDY

NEVERS

BURGUNDY

BOURBON

AUVERGNE

VELAY

Rhône River

DAUPHINE
DE VIENNOIS

GÉVAUDAN

RODEZ

Rhône

DIOIS

CASTRES

PROVENCE

NARBONNE

ROUSSILLON

SCALE IN MILES

0   50   100   150

Actual Chronology for Events in the Three Parts of Henry VI

1421
Dec. 6   Birth of Henry VI at Windsor.

1422
Aug. 31   Death of Henry V at Vincennes.
Oct. 21   Charles VI of France dies, succeeded by Charles VII.
Nov. 7   Body of Henry V lies in state in Westminster Abbey.
Nov. 9   Parliament summoned.

1423
Aug. 1   Salisbury defeats French at Cravant.

1424
Aug. 17   Bedford defeats French at Verneuil.

1425
Aug. 2   Salisbury takes Le Mans.
Oct. 1   Gloucester and Winchester clash in London.

1427
Sept. 5   Dunois, Bastard of Orléans, defeats English at Montargis.

1429
May 1-3   Joan of Arc raises the siege of Orléans.
July 17   Charles VII crowned at Reims.
Nov. 6   Henry VI crowned at Westminster.

1430
May 23   Joan of Arc captured at Compiègne.

1431
May 30   Joan of Arc burned at Rouen.
Dec. 16   Henry VI crowned in Notre Dame, Paris.

1435
Sept. 15   Death of John, Duke of Bedford.

1436   French recover Paris.

1444
May 28   Two-year Anglo-French truce signed at Tours.

1

1445
April 22   Henry VI marries Margaret of Anjou.
1448
May   French recover Maine and Anjou by mar-
            riage treaty.
1450–1454 Jack Cade's Rebellion.
1451   French conquer Guienne.
1453   English retain only Calais and Channel Is-
            lands of French possessions.
1454
March 27   Richard, Duke of York, made Protector.
1455
May 22   1st Battle of St. Albans; Yorkist victory.
1460
July 10   Battle of Northampton; Yorkist victory.
Dec. 30   Battle of Wakefield; Lancastrian victory;
            death of Duke of York.
1461
Feb. 2   Battle of Mortimer's Cross; Yorkist victory.
Feb. 17   2nd Battle of St. Albans; Lancastrian victory.
March 1   Edward, Earl of March, acclaimed King in
            London.
March 29   Battle of Towton; rout of Lancastrians.
June 28   Coronation of Edward IV; Henry VI and
            Margaret of Anjou retire to Scotland.
July 22   Death of Charles VII of France; succeeded
            by Louis XI.
1469
July 26   Battle of Banbury; victory of Warwick
            against forces of Edward IV.
1470
Oct. 13   Henry VI restored to throne.
1471
April 14   Battle of Barnet; Yorkist victory; death of
            Earl of Warwick.
May 4   Battle of Tewkesbury; decisive Yorkist vic-
            tory; death of Edward, Prince of Wales.

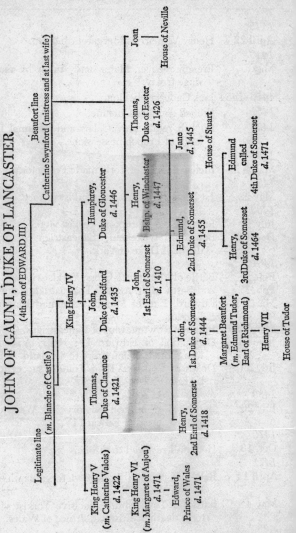

HOUSE OF LANCASTER

JOHN OF GAUNT, DUKE OF LANCASTER
(4th son of EDWARD III)

Legitimate line (*m.* Blanche of Castile)   Catherine Swynford (mistress and at last wife)   Beaufort line

King Henry IV

Thomas, Duke of Clarence *d.* 1421

John, Duke of Bedford *d.* 1435

Humphrey, Duke of Gloucester *d.* 1446

Henry, Bshp. of Winchester *d.* 1447

Thomas, Duke of Exeter *d.* 1426

Joan — House of Neville

John, 1st Earl of Somerset *d.* 1410

King Henry V (*m.* Catherine Valois) *d.* 1422

King Henry VI (*m.* Margaret of Anjou) *d.* 1471

Edward, Prince of Wales *d.* 1471

Henry, 2nd Earl of Somerset *d.* 1418

John, 1st Duke of Somerset *d.* 1444

Edmund, 2nd Duke of Somerset *d.* 1455

Jane *d.* 1445 — House of Stuart

Margaret Beaufort (*m.* Edmund Tudor, Earl of Richmond)

Henry VII

House of Tudor

Henry, 3rd Duke of Somerset *d.* 1464

Edmund called 4th Duke of Somerset *d.* 1471

HOUSE OF YORK

EDMUND OF LANGLEY, DUKE OF YORK

(5th son of EDWARD III)
(m. ISABELLA of CASTILE)

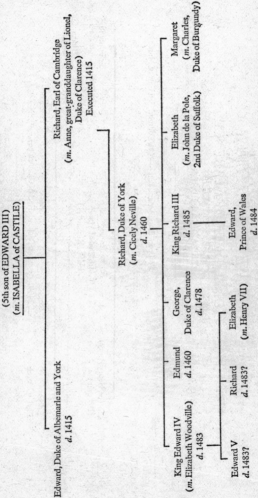

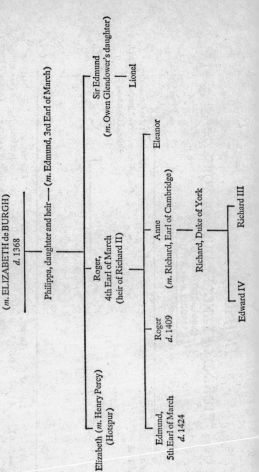

HOUSE OF MORTIMER

LIONEL, DUKE OF CLARENCE
(3rd son of EDWARD III)
(m. ELIZABETH de BURGH)
d. 1368

Philippa, daughter and heir —— (m. Edmund, 3rd Earl of March)

Elizabeth (m. Henry Percy)
(Hotspur)

Roger,
4th Earl of March
(heir of Richard II)

Sir Edmund
(m. Owen Glendower's daughter)

Lionel

Edmund,
5th Earl of March
d. 1424

Roger
d. 1409

Anne
(m. Richard, Earl of Cambridge)

Eleanor

Richard, Duke of York

Edward IV

Richard III

King Henry the Sixth.

John, Duke of Bedford, uncle to the *King* and Regent of
France.

Humphrey, Duke of Gloucester, uncle to the *King* and
Protector.

Thomas Beaufort, Duke of Exeter, great-uncle to the
King.

Henry Beaufort, great-uncle to the *King, Bishop of Winchester,* and afterward *Cardinal.*

John Beaufort, Earl, afterward *Duke, of Somerset.*

Richard Plantagenet, son of Richard, late Earl of Cambridge, afterward *Duke of York.*

Richard Beauchamp, Earl of Warwick.

Thomas Montagu, Earl of Salisbury.

William de la Pole, Earl of Suffolk.

John Talbot, afterward *Earl of Shrewsbury.*

John Talbot, his son.

Edmund Mortimer, Earl of March.

Sir John Fastolfe.

Sir William Lucy.

Sir William Glansdale.

Sir Thomas Gargrave.

Mayor of London.

Richard Woodville, Lieutenant of the Tower.

Sir Richard Vernon, of the white rose or York faction.

Basset, of the red rose or Lancaster faction.

A Lawyer.

Charles, Dauphin, and afterward *King, of France.*

Reignier, Duke of Anjou and titular *King of Naples.*

Philip, Duke of Burgundy.

John, Duke of Alençon.

John Dunois, Bastard of Orléans.

Governor of Paris.

Master Gunner of Orléans and his *Son.*

lv

General of the French forces in Bordeaux.
A French Sergeant.
A Porter.
An old Shepherd, father to *Joan la Pucelle.*

Margaret, daughter to *Reignier,* afterward married to
    King Henry.
Countess of Auvergne.
Joan la Pucelle, commonly called *Joan of Arc.*
Lords, Warders of the Tower, Mortimer's Keepers,
    Heralds, Officers, Soldiers, Messengers, Servingmen,
    Attendants; Fiends appearing to La Pucelle.
        SCENE: *England and France.*]

THE FIRST PART
OF
HENRY THE SIXTH

ACT I

I.i. The body of Henry V lies in state in West-minster Abbey. Lamentation over the King's death and praise of his deeds are interrupted by a hostile exchange between the King's brother, Gloucester, and his uncle, the Bishop of Winchester. The King's oldest brother, John, Duke of Bedford, fears that his death will have disastrous consequences for England. Bedford's words are immediately followed by messages reporting English losses in France and the defeat and capture of England's chief warrior, Lord Talbot. Bedford, as Regent of France, vows to rescue Talbot and overthrow the Dauphin. Gloucester, Protector of the realm, sets out for the Tower to survey the armament; Exeter, governor of the young King Henry VI, leaves to look after his charge. Winchester, disgruntled at having no large part to play, expresses a determination to alter this state of affairs. The opening scene epitomizes a main theme of the trilogy on Henry VI: the disorder that results from lack of a single firm hand at the helm of state.

━━━━━━━━━━━━━━━

Ent. **Bedford:** John of Lancaster, who appeared in the two parts of *Henry IV* and in *Henry V;* **Somerset:** although the Folio titles Somerset **Duke,** he did not assume the ducal title until 1443.

1. **heavens:** a reference to the dramatic practice of draping the canopy over the stage **(the heavens)** with black when a tragedy was to be performed.

3. **importing:** portending.

4. **Brandish:** flash menacingly; **tresses:** i.e., tail.

(continued on next page)

1

ACT I

Scene I. [Westminster Abbey.]

Dead march. Enter the funeral of King Henry the Fifth, attended on by the Duke of Bedford, Regent of France; the Duke of Gloucester, Protector; the Duke of Exeter; [the Earl of] Warwick; the Bishop of Winchester, and the Duke of Somerset; [Heralds, etc.]

Bed. Hung be the heavens with black, yield day
    to night!
Comets, importing change of times and states,
Brandish your crystal tresses in the sky,
And with them scourge the bad revolting stars   5
That have consented unto Henry's death!
King Henry the Fifth, too famous to live long!
England ne'er lost a king of so much worth.
  Glou. England ne'er had a king until his time:
Virtue he had, deserving to command;   10
His brandished sword did blind men with his beams;
His arms spread wider than a dragon's wings;
His sparkling eyes, replete with wrathful fire,
More dazzled and drove back his enemies

I

The word "comet" derives via Latin from the Greek *aster kometes* (long-haired star).

5. **revolting:** rebellious; **stars:** comets were visible signs of cosmic disorder, accompanying disastrous earthly events; while stars were believed actually to influence events on earth.

7. **too famous to live long:** two proverbs are suggested: that those beloved of the gods die young, and that a "wonder lasts but nine days" (compare *2 Henry VI,* [II. iv.] 72, and *3 Henry VI,* [III. ii.] 114).

10. **Virtue:** not simply moral excellence but all the qualities appropriate to man.

11. **his:** its.

＊　＊　＊

17. **lift:** lifted.

18-9. **in blood:** i.e., by emulating his deeds in renewed attacks against the French.

24. **triumphant:** triumphal, with reference to the triumphal processions of Roman generals.

35-6. **churchmen:** Gloucester hints that Winchester has prayed for Henry's death.

37. **thread of life:** referring to the control of human life by the Fates, one of whom, Klotho, spun the thread of human life, while Lachesis determined its length, and Atropos cut it to the destined length.

Than midday sun fierce bent against their faces.   15
What should I say? His deeds exceed all speech:
He ne'er lift up his hand but conquered.
 Exe. We mourn in black: why mourn we not in
  blood?
Henry is dead and never shall revive.   20
Upon a wooden coffin we attend,
And Death's dishonorable victory
We with our stately presence glorify,
Like captives bound to a triumphant car.
What! shall we curse the planets of mishap   25
That plotted thus our glory's overthrow?
Or shall we think the subtle-witted French
Conjurers and sorcerers, that, afraid of him,
By magic verses have contrived his end?
 Win. He was a king blessed of the King of Kings.   30
Unto the French the dreadful Judgment Day
So dreadful will not be as was his sight.
The battles of the Lord of hosts he fought:
The church's prayers made him so prosperous.
 Glou. The church! Where is it? Had not church-   35
  men prayed,
His thread of life had not so soon decayed.
None do you like but an effeminate prince,
Whom, like a schoolboy, you may overawe.
 Win. Gloucester, whate'er we like, thou art Pro-   40
  tector
And lookest to command the prince and realm.
Thy wife is proud: she holdeth thee in awe,
More than God or religious churchmen may.
 Glou. Name not religion, for thou lovest the flesh,   45

53. **await for:** expect.

55. **marish:** marsh.

61. **Caesar:** Caesar's metamorphosis to a blazing star is mentioned by Ovid, *Metamorphoses,* bk. xv. See illustration, p. 4. Scholars have made various conjectures of possible words to fill out this line. The break, however, may have been deliberate, to indicate interruption by a hasty messenger.

63. **Sad tidings:** historically, Henry V died in 1422, but the messenger's news anticipates English losses over a period of years: Guienne (1451), Champagne (possibly Compiègne, 1429), Orléans (1429), Reims (1429) (possibly, in view of Gloucester's reply, Rouen, 1449), Paris (1436), Patay (Poitiers in text), 1429. This is a deliberate telescoping of events for dramatic effect.

68. **corse:** corpse.

70. **lead:** the leaden lining of his coffin.

A comet with crystal tresses. From Conrad Lycosthenes, *Prodigiorum . . . chronicon* (1557).

3

And ne'er throughout the year to church thou goest
Except it be to pray against thy foes.
   Bed. Cease, cease these jars and rest your minds
     in peace.
Let's to the altar. Heralds, wait on us.   50
Instead of gold, we'll offer up our arms,
Since arms avail not, now that Henry's dead.
Posterity, await for wretched years,
When at their mothers' moist eyes babes shall suck,
Our isle be made a marish of salt tears,   55
And none but women left to wail the dead.
Henry the Fifth, thy ghost I invocate:
Prosper this realm, keep it from civil broils,
Combat with adverse planets in the heavens!
A far more glorious star thy soul will make   60
Than Julius Caesar or bright—

Enter a Messenger.

   Mess. My honorable lords, health to you all!
Sad tidings bring I to you out of France,
Of loss, of slaughter and discomfiture:
Guienne, Champagne, Reims, Orléans,   65
Paris, Gisors, Poitiers, are all quite lost.
   Bed. What sayst thou, man, before dead Henry's
     corse?
Speak softly, or the loss of those great towns
Will make him burst his lead and rise from death.   70
   Glou. Is Paris lost? Is Rouen yielded up?
If Henry were recalled to life again,

73. **These news:** *news* was originally a plural, deriving from Old French *nouveles*, Latin *nova*, meaning "new things."

79. **several:** private; individual.

83. **wanteth:** lacks. The idea is proverbial.

88. **flower-de-luces:** fleurs-de-lis, emblem of French royalty. England's coat of arms quartered fleurs-de-lis with the British symbol, lions. See the shield borne by Henry V in the illustration, p. 7.

91. **her:** the tears of all England could be meant; but this may be the Middle English *her* meaning "their."

96. **intermissive:** intermittent.

Julius Caesar's metamorphosis to a star. From Gabriele Simeoni, *La vita et Metamorfoseo d'Ovidio* (1559).

These news would cause him once more yield the
    ghost.

  Exe. How were they lost? What treachery was   75
    used?

  Mess. No treachery, but want of men and money.
Amongst the soldiers this is muttered,
That here you maintain several factions,
And whilst a field should be dispatched and fought,   80
You are disputing of your generals.
One would have ling'ring wars with little cost;
Another would fly swift, but wanteth wings;
A third thinks, without expense at all,
By guileful fair words peace may be obtained.   85
Awake, awake, English nobility!
Let not sloth dim your honors new-begot.
Cropped are the flower-de-luces in your arms;
Of England's coat one half is cut away.

  Exe. Were our tears wanting to this funeral,   90
These tidings would call forth her flowing tides.

  Bed. Me they concern: Regent I am of France.
Give me my steeled coat: I'll fight for France.
Away with these disgraceful wailing robes!
Wounds will I lend the French instead of eyes,   95
To weep their intermissive miseries.

Enter to them another Messenger.

  Mess. Lords, view these letters, full of bad mis-
    chance.
France is revolted from the English quite,
Except some petty towns of no import.   100

101. **Dauphin Charles:** the Dauphin's coronation and all of Joan of Arc's victories actually took place in 1429.

102. **Bastard of Orléans:** the illegitimate son of Charles, Duke of Orléans.

115. **dismal:** disastrous.

116. **stout:** valiant.

119. **circumstance:** details; **at large:** in full.

126. **He wanted pikes:** the passage derives from Holinshed's description of the Battle of Patay (1429): "The Englishmen had not leisure to put themselves in array, after they had put up their stakes before their archers; so that there was no remedy but to fight at adventure, . . . yet they never fled back one foot till their captain, the Lord Talbot, was sore wounded at the back and so taken."

The Dauphin Charles is crowned King in Reims;
The Bastard of Orléans with him is joined;
Reignier, Duke of Anjou, doth take his part;
The Duke of Alençon flieth to his side.   *Exit.*

  Exe. The Dauphin crowned King! All fly to him!   105
Oh, whither shall we fly from this reproach?

  Glou. We will not fly but to our enemies' throats.
Bedford, if thou be slack, I'll fight it out.

  Bed. Gloucester, why doubtst thou of my forward-
     ness?   110
An army have I mustered in my thoughts,
Wherewith already France is overrun.

Enter another Messenger.

  Mess. My gracious lords, to add to your laments,
Wherewith you now bedew King Henry's hearse,
I must inform you of a dismal fight   115
Betwixt the stout Lord Talbot and the French.

  Win. What! wherein Talbot overcame? Is't so?

  Mess. Oh, no; wherein Lord Talbot was o'erthrown.
The circumstance I'll tell you more at large.
The tenth of August last this dreadful lord,   120
Retiring from the siege of Orléans,
Having full scarce six thousand in his troop,
By three-and-twenty thousand of the French
Was round encompassed and set upon.
No leisure had he to enrank his men;   125
He wanted pikes to set before his archers;
Instead whereof sharp stakes plucked out of hedges
They pitched in the ground confusedly,

133. **stand:** stand up to.

136. **agazed:** gazing in terror; possibly a variant of "aghast."

138. **amain:** with full force of voice.

140. **sealed up:** clinched.

141. **Fastolfe:** historically the correct form of the name, which Shakespeare spells "Falstaffe." This is not the character of the Henry IV plays.

142. **vaward:** vanguard, forefront; **behind:** i.e., not in the very front ranks but placed in a position to reinforce the foremost battle line.

147. **grace:** favor.

156. **Lord Scales:** Thomas, seventh Baron Scales; **Lord Hungerford:** Sir Walter, first Baron Hungerford.

158. **there is none but I shall pay:** i.e., no one but I shall pay.

To keep the horsemen off from breaking in.
More than three hours the fight continued;   130
Where valiant Talbot above human thought
Enacted wonders with his sword and lance.
Hundreds he sent to hell, and none durst stand him;
Here, there, and everywhere, enraged, he slew.
The French exclaimed the Devil was in arms;   135
All the whole army stood agazed on him.
His soldiers, spying his undaunted spirit,
"A Talbot! a Talbot!" cried out amain
And rushed into the bowels of the battle.
Here had the conquest fully been sealed up,   140
If Sir John Fastolfe had not played the coward.
He, being in the vaward placed behind,
With purpose to relieve and follow them,
Cowardly fled, not having struck one stroke.
Hence grew the general wrack and massacre: 145
Enclosed were they with their enemies.
A base Walloon, to win the Dauphin's grace,
Thrust Talbot with a spear into the back,
Whom all France with their chief assembled strength
Durst not presume to look once in the face.   150

    Bed. Is Talbot slain? Then I will slay myself,
For living idly here in pomp and ease,
Whilst such a worthy leader, wanting aid,
Unto his dastard foemen is betrayed.

    Mess. Oh, no, he lives but is took prisoner,   155
And Lord Scales with him, and Lord Hungerford:
Most of the rest slaughtered or took likewise.

    Bed. His ransom there is none but I shall pay.
I'll hale the Dauphin headlong from his throne:

164. **St. George:** patron saint of England.

171. **watch:** guard.

173. **quell:** kill; destroy.

181. **governor:** although Gloucester was Protector of the realm, Exeter was the boy Henry's guardian.

185. **Jack-out-of-office:** a common term for one who has no official position.

187. **public weal:** the commonwealth; the state.

Henry V with a shield showing the arms of England. From John Taylor, *All the Works* (1630).

His crown shall be the ransom of my friend.   160
Four of their lords I'll change for one of ours.
Farewell, my masters; to my task will I.
Bonfires in France forthwith I am to make,
To keep our great St. George's feast withal.
Ten thousand soldiers with me I will take,   165
Whose bloody deeds shall make all Europe quake.

   Mess. So you had need; for Orléans is besieged;
The English army is grown weak and faint.
The Earl of Salisbury craveth supply,
And hardly keeps his men from mutiny,   170
Since they, so few, watch such a multitude.

   Exe. Remember, lords, your oaths to Henry sworn,
Either to quell the Dauphin utterly,
Or bring him in obedience to your yoke.

   Bed. I do remember it and here take my leave,   175
To go about my preparation.   *Exit.*

   Glou. I'll to the Tower with all the haste I can,
To view the artillery and munition;
And then I will proclaim young Henry King.   *Exit.*

   Exe. To Eltham will I, where the young King is,   180
Being ordained his special governor,
And for his safety there I'll best devise.   *Exit.*

   Win. Each hath his place and function to attend:
I am left out; for me nothing remains.
But long I will not be Jack-out-of-office!   185
The King from Eltham I intend to steal
And sit at chiefest stern of public weal.

                      Exeunt.

I.[ii.] The Dauphin and his men, attempting to rout the English besieging Orléans, are repelled with heavy losses. They are about to retreat when the Bastard of Orléans introduces Joan la Pucelle, who claims to have been ordained by Heaven to free the city and drive the English from France. When she bests Charles in single combat, he is convinced of her power and resolves to try again to raise the siege.

▬▬▬▬▬▬▬▬▬▬▬▬▬▬

1. Mars his true moving: the true motion of the planet Mars; figuratively, the favor of the god of war.

7. Otherwhiles: the sense seems to require some meaning like "while, on the other hand."

15. wont: used.

17. gall: bile; hence, hostility.

18. Nor: neither.

20. forlorn: doomed to destruction. A "forlorn hope" was a body of soldiers assigned to an advance position in the attack, whose hope of survival was slim. Charles uses the word from the English point of view, with determination to prove it wrong.

[Scene II. France. Before Orleans.]

Sound a flourish. Enter Charles, Alençon, and Reign-
ier, marching with Drum and Soldiers.

  Char. Mars his true moving, even as in the heavens
So in the earth, to this day is not known.
Late did he shine upon the English side:
Now we are victors; upon us he smiles.
What towns of any moment but we have?   5
At pleasure here we lie near Orléans;
Otherwhiles the famished English, like pale ghosts,
Faintly besiege us one hour in a month.
  Alen. They want their porridge and their fat bull
    beeves.   10
Either they must be dieted like mules,
And have their provender tied to their mouths,
Or piteous they will look, like drowned mice.
  Reign. Let's raise the siege: why live we idly here?
Talbot is taken, whom we wont to fear.   15
Remaineth none but mad-brained Salisbury;
And he may well in fretting spend his gall,
Nor men nor money hath he to make war.
  Char. Sound, sound alarum! We will rush on them.
Now for the honor of the forlorn French!   20
Him I forgive my death that killeth me
When he sees me go back one foot or fly.   *Exeunt.*
Here alarum: they are beaten back by the English
        with great loss.

31. **Olivers and Rowlands:** Rowland (or Roland), the supposed nephew of Charlemagne, and his friend Oliver, who were killed at Roncesvalles in 778, were heroes of many romances.

38-9. **hare-brained:** reckless to the point of madness, like a hare in spring.

41-2. **with their teeth/ The walls they'll tear down:** an echo of a proverb that "hunger breaks down stone walls."

43. **gimmers:** mechanism. The image suggests a clock with a mechanical man to strike the hours.

44. **still:** ever.

Enter Charles, Alençon, and Reignier.

Char. Who ever saw the like? What men have I!
Dogs! cowards! dastards! I would ne'er have fled
But that they left me 'midst my enemies.   25
   Reign. Salisbury is a desperate homicide;
He fighteth as one weary of his life.
The other lords, like lions wanting food,
Do rush upon us as their hungry prey.
   Alen. Froissart, a countryman of ours, records   30
England all Olivers and Rowlands bred
During the time Edward the Third did reign.
More truly now may this be verified;
For none but Samsons and Goliases
It sendeth forth to skirmish. One to ten!   35
Lean raw-boned rascals!—who would e'er suppose
They had such courage and audacity?
   Char. Let's leave this town; for they are hare-
        brained slaves,
And hunger will enforce them to be more eager: 40
Of old I know them; rather with their teeth
The walls they'll tear down than forsake the siege.
   Reign. I think, by some odd gimmers or device
Their arms are set, like clocks, still to strike on;
Else ne'er could they hold out so as they do.   45
By my consent, we'll even let them alone.
   Alen. Be it so.

51. **cheer:** expression.

51-2. **appalled:** dismayed.

60. **nine Sibyls:** Shakespeare confuses the nine books of the Cumaean Sibyl with the number of Sibyls of Rome; they are sometimes numbered ten, but not nine.

View of Orléans. From John Speed, *A Prospect of the Most Famous Parts of the World* (1632).

Enter the Bastard of Orléans.

  Bas. Where's the Prince Dauphin? I have news for
    him.
  Char. Bastard of Orléans, thrice welcome to us.   50
  Bas. Methinks your looks are sad, your cheer ap-
    palled.
Hath the late overthrow wrought this offense?
Be not dismayed, for succor is at hand.
A holy maid hither with me I bring,   55
Which by a vision sent to her from Heaven
Ordained is to raise this tedious siege
And drive the English forth the bounds of France.
The spirit of deep prophecy she hath,
Exceeding the nine Sibyls of old Rome: 60
What's past and what's to come she can descry.
Speak, shall I call her in? Believe my words,
For they are certain and unfallible.
  Char. Go, call her in. [*Exit Bastard.*] But first, to
    try her skill,   65
Reignier, stand thou as Dauphin in my place.
Question her proudly; let thy looks be stern.
By this means shall we sound what skill she hath.

Enter [the Bastard of Orléans, with] Joan la Pucelle.

  Reign. Fair maid, is't thou wilt do these wondrous
    feats?   70
  Puc. Reignier, is't thou that thinkest to beguile me?
Where is the Dauphin? Come, come from behind:

77. **takes upon her:** presumes.

90. **swart:** swarthy.

91. **clear:** pure.

97. **Resolve on this:** be assured.

98. **mate:** ambiguous; possibly meaning only "comrade," but anticipating the later charges against Joan's chastity.

99. **high:** haughty.

100. **proof:** test.

101. **buckle:** closely engage.

Siege artillery. From Olaus Magnus, *Historia de gentibus septentrionalibus* (1555).

I know thee well, though never seen before.
Be not amazed, there's nothing hid from me.
In private will I talk with thee apart: 75
Stand back, you lords, and give us leave awhile.
   Reign. She takes upon her bravely at first dash.
   Puc. Dauphin, I am by birth a shepherd's daughter,
My wit untrained in any kind of art.
Heaven and Our Lady gracious hath it pleased   80
To shine on my contemptible estate.
Lo, whilst I waited on my tender lambs,
And to sun's parching heat displayed my cheeks,
God's mother deigned to appear to me,
And in a vision full of majesty   85
Willed me to leave my base vocation
And free my country from calamity:
Her aid she promised and assured success.
In complete glory she revealed herself;
And, whereas I was black and swart before,   90
With those clear rays which she infused on me
That beauty am I blessed with which you see.
Ask me what question thou canst possible,
And I will answer unpremeditated.
My courage try by combat, if thou darest,   95
And thou shalt find that I exceed my sex.
Resolve on this, thou shalt be fortunate,
If thou receive me for thy warlike mate.
   Char. Thou hast astonished me with thy high terms.
Only this proof I'll of thy valor make: 100
In single combat thou shalt buckle with me;
And if thou vanquishest, thy words are true;
Otherwise I renounce all confidence.

111. **Deborah:** a prophetess of Israel, who encouraged Barak to defeat the hosts of Canaan (Judges 4). Elizabethan writers frequently equated Queen Elizabeth with Deborah in tribute to her wisdom and the moral inspiration she provided.

115. **thy desire:** amorous desire of thee.

117. **Excellent:** pre-eminent.

127. **shrives:** literally, hears confession and imposes penance (often performed wearing only a shift, or smock), but Alençon implies that Charles has stripped Joan with amorous intent.

131. **mean:** proportion; i.e., he is unreasonably long in conversation.

Amazons in battle. From Ovid, *Metamorphoses* (1509).

Puc. I am prepared. Here is my keen-edged sword,
Decked with five flower-de-luces on each side; 105
The which at Touraine, in St. Katharine's churchyard,
Out of a great deal of old iron I chose forth.

Char. Then come, o' God's name. I fear no woman.

Puc. And while I live, I'll ne'er fly from a man.

Here they fight, and Joan la Pucelle overcomes.

Char. Stay, stay thy hands! Thou art an Amazon 110
And fightest with the sword of Deborah.

Puc. Christ's Mother helps me, else I were too weak.

Char. Whoe'er helps thee, 'tis thou that must help
me:
Impatiently I burn with thy desire; 115
My heart and hands thou hast at once subdued.
Excellent Pucelle, if thy name be so,
Let me thy servant and not sovereign be:
'Tis the French Dauphin sueth to thee thus.

Puc. I must not yield to any rites of love, 120
For my profession's sacred from above.
When I have chased all thy foes from hence,
Then will I think upon a recompense.

Char. Meantime look gracious on thy prostrate
thrall. 125

Reign. My lord, methinks, is very long in talk.

Alen. Doubtless he shrives this woman to her
smock;
Else ne'er could he so long protract his speech.

Reign. Shall we disturb him, since he keeps no 130
mean?

Alen. He may mean more than we poor men do
know:

138. **recreants:** cowards.

143. **St. Martin's summer:** Indian summer; St. Martin's Day falls on November 11; **halcyon's days:** a period in the winter season when the seas are calm. According to classical legend, the kingfisher nested on the water at this season (see the story of Alcyone, Ovid, *Metamorphoses*, bk. xi).

150. **insulting:** vaunting; exulting.

151. **Caesar:** Plutarch, in his life of Julius Caesar, describes Caesar's attempt to sail from Apollonia to Brundusium in a small ship, which had to turn back because of the turbulence of the sea.

152. **Mahomet:** many Elizabethan writers mention the dove that Mahomet trained to eat grain from his ear, claiming that the dove was reporting to him the word of God.

154. **Helen:** St. Helena allegedly discovered fragments of the True Cross.

155. **St. Philip's daughters:** the four daughters of St. Philip had the gift of prophecy (Acts 21:9).

162. **Presently:** at once.

These women are shrewd tempters with their tongues.
 Reign. My lord, where are you? What devise you 135
  on?
Shall we give over Orléans, or no?
 Puc. Why, no, I say, distrustful recreants!
Fight till the last gasp. I will be your guard.
 Char. What she says I'll confirm: we'll fight it out. 140
 Puc. Assigned am I to be the English scourge.
This night the siege assuredly I'll raise.
Expect St. Martin's summer, halcyon's days,
Since I have entered into these wars.
Glory is like a circle in the water,   145
Which never ceaseth to enlarge itself
Till by broad spreading it disperse to nought.
With Henry's death the English circle ends:
Dispersed are the glories it included.
Now am I like that proud insulting ship   150
Which Caesar and his fortune bare at once.
 Char. Was Mahomet inspired with a dove?
Thou with an eagle art inspired then.
Helen, the mother of great Constantine,
Nor yet St. Philip's daughters, were like thee.   155
Bright star of Venus, fall'n down on the earth,
How may I reverently worship thee enough?
 Alen. Leave off delays, and let us raise the siege.
 Reign. Woman, do what thou canst to save our
  honors: 160
Drive them from Orléans and be immortalized.
 Char. Presently we'll try. Come, let's away about it.
No prophet will I trust, if she prove false.
               Exeunt.

I.[iii.] Gloucester is denied entrance to the Tower of London by order of the Bishop of Winchester, who shortly appears with his retainers. Gloucester and Winchester exchange insults, and Gloucester attempts to remove Winchester forcibly, while his men drive off the Bishop's retainers. The fracas is finally stopped by the Mayor of London. Gloucester and Winchester obey the Mayor's order to go home peacefully, but their mutual hatred has been intensified and they both vow revenge.

〰〰〰〰〰〰〰〰〰〰〰〰

2. **conveyance:** theft of armor and weapons from the Tower.

17. **warrantise:** guarantee of immunity from punishment.

14

[Scene III. London. Before the Tower.]

Enter Gloucester, with his Servingmen [in blue coats].

Glou. I am come to survey the Tower this day:
Since Henry's death, I fear there is conveyance.
Where be these warders, that they wait not here?
Open the gates: 'tis Gloucester that calls.
   1. Ward. [*Within*] Who's there that knocks so im-   5
    periously?
   1. Serv. It is the noble Duke of Gloucester.
   2. Ward. [*Within*] Whoe'er he be, you may not be
    let in.
   1. Serv. Villains, answer you so the Lord Protector? 10
   1. Ward. [*Within*] The Lord protect him! So we
    answer him:
We do no otherwise than we are willed.
   Glou. Who willed you? or whose will stands but
    mine? 15
There's none Protector of the realm but I.
Break up the gates, I'll be your warrantise.
Shall I be flouted thus by dunghill grooms?
Gloucester's men rush at the Tower Gates, and Wood-
              ville, the Lieutenant, speaks within.
   Wood. What noise is this? What traitors have we
    here? 20
   Glou. Lieutenant, is it you whose voice I hear?
Open the gates: here's Gloucester that would enter.
   Wood. Have patience, noble Duke. I may not open:

24. **Cardinal:** Winchester was nominated Cardinal of St. Eusebius by the Pope in 1426.

30. **brook:** endure.

38. **Peeled:** shaven; tonsured.

40. **proditor:** traitor.

44. **whores:** referring to the notorious brothels which stood on lands belonging to the Bishop of Winchester in Southwark, south of the Thames, in Shakespeare's time.

45. **canvass:** toss as in a canvas.

48. **This be Damascus:** let this be Damascus (supposed site of Cain's murder of Abel).

The Cardinal of Winchester forbids.
From him I have express commandement   25
That thou nor none of thine shall be let in.
  Glou. Faint-hearted Woodville, prizest him 'fore
    me?
Arrogant Winchester, that haughty prelate,
Whom Henry, our late sovereign, ne'er could brook?   30
Thou art no friend to God or to the King.
Open the gates, or I'll shut thee out shortly.
  Serv. Open the gates unto the Lord Protector,
Or we'll burst them open, if that you come not
    quickly.   35

*Enter to the Protector at the Tower gates Winchester
and his men in tawny coats.*

  Win. How now, ambitious Humphrey! What means
    this?
  Glou. Peeled priest, dost thou command me to be
    shut out?
  Win. I do, thou most usurping proditor,   40
And not Protector, of the King or realm.
  Glou. Stand back, thou manifest conspirator,
Thou that contrivedst to murder our dead lord;
Thou that givest whores indulgences to sin.
I'll canvass thee in thy broad Cardinal's hat,   45
If thou proceed in this thy insolence.
  Win. Nay, stand thou back: I will not budge a foot.
This be Damascus, be thou cursed Cain,
To slay thy brother Abel, if thou wilt.
  Glou. I will not slay thee, but I'll drive thee back.   50

51. **bearing cloth:** a cloth in which an infant was wrapped to be carried to its christening.

55. **privileged:** as a royal stronghold, the Tower precincts were **privileged** against disorders, which were liable to severe punishment.

59. **dignities:** dignitaries.

63. **Winchester goose:** denizen of a brothel on Winchester's lands; prostitute.

67-8. **magistrates:** government officials.

69. **contumeliously:** in a manner showing lack of respect (for the law of the land).

73. **distrained:** seized (a legal term).

75. **motions:** urges.

76. **free:** generous.

Thy scarlet robes as a child's bearing cloth
I'll use to carry thee out of this place.

   Win. Do what thou darest, I beard thee to thy face.

   Glou. What! am I dared and bearded to my face?
Draw, men, for all this privileged place: 55
Blue coats to tawny coats! Priest, beware your beard:
I mean to tug it and to cuff you soundly.
Under my feet I stamp thy Cardinal's hat.
In spite of Pope or dignities of church,
Here by the cheeks I'll drag thee up and down.   60

   Win. Gloucester, thou wilt answer this before the
     Pope.

   Glou. Winchester goose, I cry, a rope! a rope!
Now beat them hence: why do you let them stay?
Thee I'll chase hence, thou wolf in sheep's array.   65
Out, tawny coats! out, scarlet hypocrite!

*Here Gloucester's men beat out the Cardinal's men,
and enter in the hurly-burly the Mayor of London
                        and his Officers.*

   May. Fie, lords! that you, being supreme magis-
     trates,
Thus contumeliously should break the peace!

   Glou. Peace, Mayor! thou knowst little of my   70
     wrongs.
Here's Beaufort, that regards nor God nor King,
Hath here distrained the Tower to his use.

   Win. Here's Gloucester, a foe to citizens,
One that still motions war and never peace,
O'ercharging your free purses with large fines;   75
That seeks to overthrow religion,
Because he is Protector of the realm,

93. **break:** reveal.

96. **clubs:** the weapon of the City's apprentices when summoned to disperse a riot.

98-9. **Thou dost but what thou mayst:** Gloucester expresses reluctant submission. The Lord Mayor's authority within the City of London had to be respected even by one as powerful as the Protector of the realm.

100. **Abominable:** inhuman; the word was incorrectly conceived as deriving from *ab homines*, "away from man," instead of from *abominabilis*, "accursed."

103. **should such stomachs bear:** should display so much hostility. The Mayor expresses astonishment, not approval of their behavior.

And would have armor here out of the Tower,
To crown himself King and suppress the Prince.   80
    Glou. I will not answer thee with words, but blows.
                            Here they skirmish again.
    May. Nought rests for me in this tumultuous strife
But to make open proclamation:
Come, officer, as loud as e'er thou canst;
Cry.   85
    Off. [*Reads*] "All manner of men assembled here in
arms this day against God's peace and the King's, we
charge and command you, in His Highness' name, to
repair to your several dwelling places and not to wear,
handle, or use any sword, weapon, or dagger, hence-   90
forward, upon pain of death."
    Glou. Cardinal, I'll be no breaker of the law:
But we shall meet and break our minds at large.
    Win. Gloucester, we'll meet, to thy cost, be sure:
Thy heartblood I will have for this day's work.   95
    May. I'll call for clubs, if you will not away.
This Cardinal's more haughty than the Devil.
    Glou. Mayor, farewell. Thou dost but what thou
    mayst.
    Win. Abominable Gloucester, guard thy head;   100
For I intend to have it ere long.
Exeunt, [*severally, Gloucester and Winchester with
                            their Servingmen*].
    May. See the coast cleared, and then we will depart.
Good God, these nobles should such stomachs bear!
I myself fight not once in forty year.
                                        Exeunt.

I.[iv.] The Master Gunner of Orléans sets his son to watch an opportunity to fire a cannon at the English in a tower near the city walls. When Talbot appears on the tower with Salisbury, Sir William Glansdale, and Sir Thomas Gargrave, the boy fires, killing Gargrave and mortally wounding Salisbury. Fresh on the heels of this disaster comes word that the French are about to renew their attack. Talbot is resolved to emulate Salisbury's past feats by destroying La Pucelle and the Dauphin.

|||||||||||||||||||||||||||||||||||||

9. **grace:** favor; honor.
10. **espials:** spies.
12. **Wont:** are accustomed.
13. **overpeer:** look down upon.
16. **intercept:** prevent; **inconvenience:** misfortune.

[Scene IV. Orléans.]

Enter, [on the walls,] the Master Gunner of Orléans
and his Boy.

M. Gun. Sirrah, thou knowst how Orléans is be-
    sieged,
And how the English have the suburbs won.
  Boy. Father, I know, and oft have shot at them,
Howe'er unfortunate I missed my aim.   5
  M. Gun. But now thou shalt not. Be thou ruled by
    me.
Chief Master Gunner am I of this town;
Something I must do to procure me grace.
The Prince's espials have informed me   10
How the English, in the suburbs close entrenched,
Wont through a secret grate of iron bars
In yonder tower to overpeer the city
And thence discover how with most advantage
They may vex us with shot or with assault.   15
To intercept this inconvenience,
A piece of ordnance 'gainst it I have placed;
And even these three days have I watched
If I could see them.
Now do thou watch, for I can stay no longer.   20
If thou spyest any, run and bring me word,
And thou shalt find me at the Governor's.   *Exit.*
  Boy. Father, I warrant you; take you no care:

36. **In fine:** finally.
40. **entertained:** received; treated.
41. **contumelious:** contemptuous.

I'll never trouble you, if I may spy them.   *Exit.*

*Enter, on the turrets, Salisbury and Talbot, with
[Sir William Glansdale, Sir Thomas Gargrave, and]
others.*

    Sal. Talbot, my life, my joy, again returned!   25
How wert thou handled being prisoner?
Or by what means gotst thou to be released?
Discourse, I prithee, on this turret's top.
    Tal. The Duke of Bedford had a prisoner
Called the brave Lord Ponton de Santrailles;   30
For him was I exchanged and ransomed.
But with a baser man of arms by far
Once in contempt they would have bartered me:
Which I, disdaining, scorned, and craved death
Rather than I would be so vile esteemed.   35
In fine, redeemed I was as I desired.
But, oh! the treacherous Fastolfe wounds my heart,
Whom with my bare fists I would execute,
If I now had him brought into my power.
    Sal. Yet tellst thou not how thou wert entertained.   40
    Tal. With scoffs and scorns and contumelious
    taunts.
In open market place produced they me,
To be a public spectacle to all.
Here, said they, is the terror of the French,   45
The scarecrow that affrights our children so.
Then broke I from the officers that led me
And with my nails digged stones out of the ground,
To hurl at the beholders of my shame.

55. **spurn:** kick; **adamant:** an imaginary stone of impenetrable hardness; the word was also sometimes applied to the diamond.

57. **every minute while:** constantly.

Ent. 59. **linstock:** a stick used to light a cannon; see illustration, below.

67. **express:** exact.

Lighting a cannon. From Edward Webbe, *The Rare and Most Wonderful Things* (1590; reprint).

My grisly countenance made others fly;   50
None durst come near for fear of sudden death.
In iron walls they deemed me not secure;
So great fear of my name 'mongst them was spread
That they supposed I could rend bars of steel
And spurn in pieces posts of adamant: 55
Wherefore a guard of chosen shot I had,
That walked about me every minute while;
And if I did but stir out of my bed,
Ready they were to shoot me to the heart.

Enter the Boy with a linstock.

Sal. I grieve to hear what torments you endured,   60
But we will be revenged sufficiently.
Now it is suppertime in Orléans.
Here, through this grate, I count each one
And view the Frenchmen how they fortify.
Let us look in; the sight will much delight thee.   65
Sir Thomas Gargrave and Sir William Glansdale,
Let me have your express opinions
Where is best place to make our battery next.
    Gar. I think, at the north gate, for there stands
        lords.   70
    Glan. And I, here, at the bulwark of the bridge.
    Tal. For aught I see, this city must be famished,
Or with light skirmishes enfeebled.
Here they shoot, and Salisbury [and Gargrave] fall
                                                down.
    Sal. O Lord, have mercy on us, wretched sinners!
    Gar. O Lord, have mercy on me, woeful man!   75

79. **mirror:** model.

92. **wants:** lacks.

101. **Plantagenet:** the traditional name applied to the descendants of Henry II, probably here a tribute to Salisbury's nobility of nature. Shakespeare apparently confuses the dying man, a Montagu, with the Salisbury of *Henry VI, Part 2*, Richard Neville, a descendant of John of Gaunt. The Salisbury title reverted to Neville through his marriage with the deceased Earl's only child, Alice Montagu.

    Tal. What chance is this that suddenly hath crossed
       us?
Speak, Salisbury; at least, if thou canst, speak:
How farest thou, mirror of all martial men?
One of thy eyes and thy cheek's side struck off!   80
Accursed tower! accursed fatal hand,
That hath contrived this woeful tragedy!
In thirteen battles Salisbury o'ercame;
Henry the Fifth he first trained to the wars;
Whilst any trump did sound or drum struck up,   85
His sword did ne'er leave striking in the field.
Yet livest thou, Salisbury? Though thy speech doth
       fail,
One eye thou hast, to look to Heaven for grace.
The sun with one eye vieweth all the world.   90
Heaven, be thou gracious to none alive,
If Salisbury wants mercy at thy hands!
Sir Thomas Gargrave, hast thou any life?
Speak unto Talbot; nay, look up to him.
Bear hence his body; I will help to bury it.   95
Salisbury, cheer thy spirit with this comfort;
Thou shalt not die whiles—
He beckons with his hand and smiles on me,
As who should say, "When I am dead and gone,
Remember to avenge me on the French."   100
Plantagenet, I will; and like thee, Nero,
Play on the lute, beholding the towns burn.
Wretched shall France be only in my name.
       Here an alarum, and it thunders and lightens.
What stir is this? What tumult's in the heavens?
Whence cometh this alarum and the noise?   105

106-7. **gathered head:** assembled an army prepared to attack.

114. **Pucelle or puzzel:** maid or harlot; **dolphin:** the usual English form of "dauphin." The **dolphin** was regarded as a noble fish, while the **dogfish** was despised.

117. **Convey me:** convey for me; the ethical dative construction.

⁚⁚⁚

I.[v.] The English troops are routed by the French under the leadership of La Pucelle and the Dauphin. Talbot and the maid fight, and the seasoned warrior finds he cannot overcome her. La Pucelle then leads her men into the town, and Talbot is left to lament his countrymen's ignominious defeat.

⁚⁚⁚⁚⁚⁚⁚⁚⁚⁚⁚⁚⁚⁚⁚⁚⁚⁚⁚⁚⁚⁚⁚⁚⁚⁚⁚⁚⁚⁚⁚⁚

1. **valor:** not "bravery" but "value," approximately equivalent to **strength** and **force.**

Enter a Messenger.

Mess. My lord, my lord, the French have gathered
    head.
The Dauphin, with one Joan la Pucelle joined,
A holy prophetess new risen up,
Is come with a great power to raise the siege.   110
      Here Salisbury lifteth himself up and groans.
  Tal. Hear, hear how dying Salisbury doth groan!
It irks his heart he cannot be revenged.
Frenchmen, I'll be a Salisbury to you.
Pucelle or puzzel, dolphin or dogfish,
Your hearts I'll stamp out with my horse's heels,   115
And make a quagmire of your mingled brains.
Convey me Salisbury into his tent,
And then we'll try what these dastard Frenchmen
    dare.

                      Alarum. Exeunt.

[Scene V. Orléans.]

*Here an alarum again and Talbot pursueth the Dau-
phin and driveth him: then enter Joan la Pucelle,
driving Englishmen before her, [and exit after them]:
        then enter Talbot.*

  Tal. Where is my strength, my valor, and my force?
Our English troops retire, I cannot stay them:
A woman clad in armor chaseth them.

6. **on:** from. It was believed that a witch could not harm one who drew blood from her.

22. **Hannibal:** referring to Hannibal's trick of rigging burning torches on the horns of oxen and driving them before his men.

23. **lists:** pleases.

30. **soil:** birthright; **give:** display (in the coat of arms).

Enter La Pucelle.

Here, here she comes. I'll have a bout with thee;
Devil or Devil's dam, I'll conjure thee.   5
Blood will I draw on thee—thou art a witch—
And straightway give thy soul to him thou servest.

  Puc. Come, come, 'tis only I that must disgrace
    thee.   *Here they fight.*

  Tal. Heavens, can you suffer hell so to prevail?   10
My breast I'll burst with straining of my courage
And from my shoulders crack my arms asunder,
But I will chastise this high-minded strumpet.
                    They fight again.

  Puc. Talbot, farewell; thy hour is not yet come:
I must go victual Orléans forthwith.   15
    A short alarum: then enter the town with soldiers.
O'ertake me, if thou canst: I scorn thy strength.
Go, go, cheer up thy hungry-starved men;
Help Salisbury to make his testament.
This day is ours, as many more shall be.   *Exit.*

  Tal. My thoughts are whirled like a potter's wheel: 20
I know not where I am, nor what I do.
A witch, by fear, not force, like Hannibal,
Drives back our troops and conquers as she lists.
So bees with smoke and doves with noisome stench
Are from their hives and houses driven away.   25
They called us for our fierceness English dogs;
Now, like to whelps, we crying run away.
                      A short alarum.
Hark, countrymen! either renew the fight,
Or tear the lions out of England's coat;
Renounce your soil, give sheep in lion's stead.   30

I.[vi.] Within the city of Orléans, La Pucelle orders the French colors placed on the walls to signify their firm possession. The Dauphin lavishes praise on the maid for her accomplishment and prophesies that she will replace St. Denis as the patron saint of France.

〰〰〰〰〰〰〰〰〰〰〰

1. **Advance:** raise; **colors:** flags.

4. **Astraea's daughter:** Astraea was goddess of justice in the Golden Age, according to Greek mythology, who fled the earth in horror at man's wickedness in the Iron Age and became the constellation Virgo.

6. **Adonis' garden:** Shakespeare probably knew the Garden of Adonis as described in Edmund Spenser's *Faerie Queene*, bk. III, canto vi, where all manner of plants grew naturally without cultivation.

The constellation Virgo (the Virgin). From Hyginus, *Fabularum liber* (1535).

Sheep run not half so treacherous from the wolf,
Or horse or oxen from the leopard,
As you fly from your oft subdued slaves.
　　　　　　　　Alarum. Here another skirmish.
It will not be. Retire into your trenches.
You all consented unto Salisbury's death,　　　　35
For none would strike a stroke in his revenge.
Pucelle is entered into Orléans,
In spite of us or aught that we could do.
Oh, would I were to die with Salisbury!
The shame hereof will make me hide my head.　　40
　　　　　　　　Exit Talbot. Alarum; retreat.

[Scene VI. Orléans.]

*Flourish. Enter, on the walls, La Pucelle, Dauphin
[Charles], Reignier, Alençon, and Soldiers.*

　Puc. Advance our waving colors on the walls:
Rescued is Orléans from the English.
Thus Joan la Pucelle hath performed her word.
　Char. Divinest creature, Astraea's daughter,
How shall I honor thee for this success?　　　　5
Thy promises are like Adonis' garden,
That one day bloomed and fruitful were the next.
France, triumph in thy glorious prophetess!
Recovered is the town of Orléans:

22. **pyramis:** pyramid.

23. **Rhodope:** Rhodope, or Rhodopis, was a Greek courtesan whom some ancient writers credited with the building of the third pyramid.

26. **coffer of Darius:** Plutarch refers to the coffer of the Persian king Darius, in which Alexander the Great thought the works of Homer deserved to be kept.

29. **St. Denis:** patron saint of France.

Charles VII of France. From Bernardo Giunti, *Cronica breve de i fatti illustri de re di Francia* (1588).

More blessed hap did ne'er befall our state.   10
   Reign. Why ring not out the bells aloud throughout
    the town?
Dauphin, command the citizens make bonfires
And feast and banquet in the open streets,
To celebrate the joy that God hath given us.   15
   Alen. All France will be replete with mirth and joy,
When they shall hear how we have played the men.
   Char. 'Tis Joan, not we, by whom the day is won;
For which I will divide my crown with her,
And all the priests and friars in my realm   20
Shall in procession sing her endless praise.
A statelier pyramis to her I'll rear
Than Rhodope's of Memphis ever was.
In memory of her when she is dead,
Her ashes, in an urn more precious   25
Then the rich-jeweled coffer of Darius,
Transported shall be at high festivals
Before the kings and queens of France.
No longer on St. Denis will we cry,
But Joan la Pucelle shall be France's saint.   30
Come in, and let us banquet royally,
After this golden day of victory.
                     Flourish. Exeunt.

THE FIRST PART
OF
HENRY THE SIXTH

ACT II

II.i. Talbot, Bedford, and the Duke of Burgundy, with troops, scale the walls of Orléans and force the Dauphin, La Pucelle, and the French leaders to fly. The men accuse each other of negligent care of their respective quarters, but La Pucelle brushes aside the question of blame and declares that they must concentrate upon getting the better of the English. As she finishes speaking, an English soldier disperses them with the Talbot battle cry.

⁗⁗⁗⁗⁗⁗⁗⁗⁗⁗⁗⁗⁗⁗⁗

3. **apparent:** unmistakable.
4. **court of guard:** guard headquarters.
6. **servitors:** servants.
9. **redoubted:** formidable; fearsome.
12. **secure:** overconfident; thus, off their guard.
15. **quittance:** requite; repay.

ACT II

Scene I. [Before Orléans.]

Enter a Sergeant of a band, with two Sentinels.

Serg. Sirs, take your places and be vigilant.
If any noise or soldier you perceive
Near to the walls, by some apparent sign
Let us have knowledge at the court of guard.
Sen. Sergeant, you shall. [*Exit Sergeant.*] Thus are   5
    poor servitors,
When others sleep upon their quiet beds,
Constrained to watch in darkness, rain, and cold.

*Enter Talbot, Bedford, Burgundy, [and forces,] with
scaling ladders, their drums beating a dead march.*

Tal. Lord Regent, and redoubted Burgundy,
By whose approach the regions of Artois,   10
Walloon, and Picardy are friends to us,
This happy night the Frenchmen are secure,
Having all day caroused and banqueted.
Embrace we then this opportunity,
As fitting best to quittance their deceit,   15

26

18. **fame:** reputation.
28. **practice:** plot.

Scaling ladders at a siege. From Olaus Magnus, *Historia de gentibus septentrionalibus* (1555).

Contrived by art and baleful sorcery.

Bed. Coward of France! How much he wrongs his
    fame,

Despairing of his own arm's fortitude,

To join with witches and the help of hell!   20

Bur. Traitors have never other company.

But what's that Pucelle whom they term so pure?

Tal. A maid, they say.

Bed.   A maid! and be so martial!

Bur. Pray God she prove not masculine ere long,   25

If underneath the standard of the French

She carry armor as she hath begun.

Tal. Well, let them practice and converse with
    spirits.

God is our fortress, in whose conquering name   30

Let us resolve to scale their flinty bulwarks.

Bed. Ascend, brave Talbot: we will follow thee.

Tal. Not all together. Better far, I guess,

That we do make our entrance several ways;

That, if it chance the one of us do fail,   35

The other yet may rise against their force.

Bed. Agreed: I'll to yond corner.

Bur.   And I to this.

Tal. And here will Talbot mount, or make his grave.

Now, Salisbury, for thee, and for the right   40

Of English Henry, shall this night appear

How much in duty I am bound to both.

Sen. Arm! arm! the enemy doth make assault!

[*The English, scaling the walls,*] cry "St. George," "A
                Talbot."

46. **trow:** declare.
54. **sped:** succeeded (in escaping).
57. **flatter us:** give us false encouragement.
60. **Wherefore:** why.

*The French leap over the walls in their shirts. Enter,
several ways, Bastard, Alençon, Reignier, half ready,
and half unready.*

Alen. How now, my lords! What, all unready so?
Bas. Unready! ay, and glad we 'scaped so well.   45
Reign. 'Twas time, I trow, to wake and leave our
    beds,
Hearing alarums at our chamber doors.
Alen. Of all exploits since first I followed arms,
Ne'er heard I of a warlike enterprise   50
More venturous or desperate than this.
Bas. I think this Talbot be a fiend of hell.
Reign. If not of hell, the Heavens, sure, favor him.
Alen. Here cometh Charles. I marvel how he sped.
Bas. Tut, holy Joan was his defensive guard.   55

Enter Charles and La Pucelle.

Char. Is this thy cunning, thou deceitful dame?
Didst thou at first, to flatter us withal,
Make us partakers of a little gain,
That now our loss might be ten times so much?
Puc. Wherefore is Charles impatient with his   60
    friend?
At all times will you have my power alike?
Sleeping or waking must I still prevail,
Or will you blame and lay the fault on me?
Improvident soldiers! had your watch been good,   65
This sudden mischief never could have fall'n.
Char. Duke of Alençon, this was your default,

83. rests: remains.

That, being captain of the watch tonight,
Did look no better to that weighty charge.

  Alen. Had all your quarters been as safely kept 70
As that whereof I had the government,
We had not been thus shamefully surprised.

  Bas. Mine was secure.

  Reign.   And so was mine, my lord.

  Char. And, for myself, most part of all this night, 75
Within her quarter and mine own precinct,
I was employed in passing to and fro,
About relieving of the sentinels.
Then how or which way should they first break in?

  Puc. Question, my lords, no further of the case, 80
How or which way. 'Tis sure they found some place
But weakly guarded, where the breach was made.
And now there rests no other shift but this,
To gather our soldiers, scattered and dispersed,
And lay new platforms to endamage them. 85

*Alarum. Enter [an English] Soldier, crying, "A Tal-
bot! a Talbot!" They fly, leaving their clothes behind.*

  Sol. I'll be so bold to take what they have left.
The cry of "Talbot" serves me for a sword;
For I have loaden me with many spoils,
Using no other weapon but his name.

              Exit.

II.[ii.] Within the town of Orléans, Talbot orders the body of Salisbury placed in the market square. A messenger brings him an invitation from the Countess of Auvergne to visit her castle. Talbot is touched at this kindness and accepts, but he issues secret instructions to one of his captains before setting out.

▬▬▬▬▬▬▬▬▬▬▬▬▬▬▬

2. **pitchy:** black.
5. **advance:** place on high.
19. **muse:** wonder.

[Scene II. Orléans. Within the town.]

Enter Talbot, Bedford, Burgundy, [a Captain, and others].

Bed. The day begins to break, and night is fled,
Whose pitchy mantle overveiled the earth.
Here sound retreat and cease our hot pursuit.
         Retreat [sounded].
 Tal. Bring forth the body of old Salisbury
And here advance it in the market place,   5
The middle center of this cursed town.
Now have I paid my vow unto his soul;
For every drop of blood was drawn from him
There hath at least five Frenchmen died tonight.
And that hereafter ages may behold   10
What ruin happened in revenge of him,
Within their chiefest temple I'll erect
A tomb, wherein his corpse shall be interred;
Upon the which, that everyone may read,
Shall be engraved the sack of Orléans,   15
The treacherous manner of his mournful death,
And what a terror he had been to France.
But, lords, in all our bloody massacre,
I muse we met not with the Dauphin's Grace,
His newcome champion, virtuous Joan of Arc,   20
Nor any of his false confederates.
 Bed. 'Tis thought, Lord Talbot, when the fight
  began,

29. **trull:** harlot.
34. **power:** troops.
35. **train:** company.
42. **vouchsafe:** condescend.

Roused on the sudden from their drowsy beds,
They did amongst the troops of armed men   25
Leap o'er the walls for refuge in the field.

   Bur. Myself, as far as I could well discern
For smoke and dusky vapors of the night,
Am sure I scared the Dauphin and his trull,
When arm in arm they both came swiftly running,   30
Like to a pair of loving turtledoves
That could not live asunder day or night.
After that things are set in order here,
We'll follow them with all the power we have.

Enter a Messenger.

   Mess. All hail, my lords! Which of this princely train   35
Call ye the warlike Talbot, for his acts
So much applauded through the realm of France?

   Tal. Here is the Talbot. Who would speak with
     him?

   Mess. The virtuous lady, Countess of Auvergne,   40
With modesty admiring thy renown,
By me entreats, great lord, thou wouldst vouchsafe
To visit her poor castle where she lies,
That she may boast she hath beheld the man
Whose glory fills the world with loud report.   45

   Bur. Is it even so? Nay, then, I see our wars
Will turn unto a peaceful comic sport,
When ladies crave to be encountered with.
You may not, my lord, despise her gentle suit.

   Tal. Ne'er trust me then; for when a world of men   50
Could not prevail with all their oratory,

60. **prove:** try.

63. **mean accordingly:** intend to act in accordance.

<hr>

II.[iii.] The Countess of Auvergne, who has planned to capture the renowned Talbot, greets him with insults, but Talbot reveals that, suspecting treachery, he had brought with him a body of soldiers. When the Countess begs forgiveness, Talbot declares that a taste of her food and wine will wipe out the insult.

<hr>

1. **gave in charge:** ordered.

6. **Tomyris:** queen of a Scythian tribe, who cut off the head of Cyrus, founder of the Persian empire, in the sixth century B.C.

7. **rumor:** report; reputation.

9. **Fain:** eagerly.

10. **censure:** opinion, good or bad.

Yet hath a woman's kindness overruled.
And therefore tell her I return great thanks
And in submission will attend on her.
Will not your Honors bear me company?   55
    Bed. No, truly, 'tis more than manners will;
And I have heard it said, unbidden guests
Are often welcomest when they are gone.
    Tal. Well then, alone, since there's no remedy,
I mean to prove this lady's courtesy.   60
Come hither, captain. (*Whispers.*) You perceive my
    mind?
    Capt. I do, my lord, and mean accordingly.
                                        Exeunt.

[Scene III. Auvergne. The Countess' castle.]

Enter Countess [and her Porter].

    Count. Porter, remember what I gave in charge;
And when you have done so, bring the keys to me.
    Port. Madam, I will.   *Exit.*
    Count. The plot is laid. If all things fall out right,
I shall as famous be by this exploit   5
As Scythian Tomyris by Cyrus' death.
Great is the rumor of this dreadful knight
And his achievements of no less account.
Fain would mine eyes be witness with mine ears,
To give their censure of these rare reports.   10

21. **aspect:** glance.
24. **writhled:** wrinkled.
28. **sort:** choose.
31. **craves:** desires; requests.
33. **Marry:** an interjection equivalent to "to tell the truth" (from "by the Virgin Mary").

Tomyris and Cyrus. From *Le microcosme* (n.d.).

Enter Messenger and Talbot.

Mess. Madam,
According as your Ladyship desired,
By message craved, so is Lord Talbot come.
   Count. And he is welcome. What! is this the man?
   Mess. Madam, it is.   15
   Count.   Is this the scourge of France?
Is this the Talbot, so much feared abroad
That with his name the mothers still their babes?
I see report is fabulous and false.
I thought I should have seen some Hercules,   20
A second Hector, for his grim aspect
And large proportion of his strong-knit limbs.
Alas, this is a child, a silly dwarf!
It cannot be this weak and writhled shrimp
Should strike such terror to his enemies.   25
   Tal. Madam, I have been bold to trouble you;
But since your Ladyship is not at leisure,
I'll sort some other time to visit you.
   Count. What means he now? Go ask him whither
     he goes.   30
   Mess. Stay, my Lord Talbot; for my lady craves
To know the cause of your abrupt departure.
   Tal. Marry, for that she's in a wrong belief,
I go to certify her Talbot's here.

38. **trained:** lured.
39. **shadow:** image.
45. **captivate:** in captivity.
49. **fond:** foolish.
60. **pitch:** height.
62. **merchant:** fellow (contemptuous); **nonce:** time being; this occasion.

Enter Porter with keys.

Count. If thou be he, then art thou prisoner.   35
Tal. Prisoner! to whom?
Count.   To me, bloodthirsty lord;
And for that cause I trained thee to my house.
Long time thy shadow hath been thrall to me,
For in my gallery thy picture hangs: 40
But now the substance shall endure the like,
And I will chain these legs and arms of thine,
That hast by tyranny these many years
Wasted our country, slain our citizens,
And sent our sons and husbands captivate.   45
    Tal. Ha, ha, ha!
    Count. Laughest thou, wretch? Thy mirth shall turn
        to moan.
    Tal. I laugh to see your Ladyship so fond
To think that you have aught but Talbot's shadow   50
Whereon to practice your severity.
    Count. Why, art not thou the man?
    Tal.   I am indeed.
    Count. Then have I substance too.
    Tal. No, no, I am but shadow of myself.   55
You are deceived, my substance is not here;
For what you see is but the smallest part
And least proportion of humanity.
I tell you, madam, were the whole frame here,
It is of such a spacious lofty pitch,   60
Your roof were not sufficient to contain 't.
    Count. This is a riddling merchant for the nonce;

70. **subverts:** ruins; razes.
73. **fame:** rumor; **bruited:** reported.
84. **cates:** delicacies.
85. **soldiers' stomachs always serve them well:** soldiers always have good appetites and courage— another meaning of **stomach.**

He will be here, and yet he is not here.
How can these contrarieties agree?

    Tal. That will I show you presently. *Winds his horn.*   65

Drums strike up: a peal of ordnance. Enter Soldiers.

How say you, madam? Are you now persuaded
That Talbot is but shadow of himself?
These are his substance, sinews, arms, and strength,
With which he yoketh your rebellious necks,
Razeth your cities, and subverts your towns,   70
And in a moment makes them desolate.

    Count. Victorious Talbot! Pardon my abuse.
I find thou art no less than fame hath bruited
And more than may be gathered by thy shape.
Let my presumption not provoke thy wrath;   75
For I am sorry that with reverence
I did not entertain thee as thou art.

    Tal. Be not dismayed, fair lady; nor misconstrue
The mind of Talbot, as you did mistake
The outward composition of his body.   80
What you have done hath not offended me;
Nor other satisfaction do I crave
But only, with your patience, that we may
Taste of your wine and see what cates you have;
For soldiers' stomachs always serve them well.   85

    Count. With all my heart, and think me honored
To feast so great a warrior in my house.

                              Exeunt.

II.[iv.] Richard Plantagenet and the Earl of Somerset seek to resolve a quarrel over a point of law. Plantagenet proposes that those who think him right indicate their position by plucking after him a white rose from a nearby bush. Somerset picks a red rose and bids his supporters do the same. Warwick and Vernon pick white roses; the other man present, the Earl of Suffolk, picks a red rose. Somerset calls Plantagenet a yeoman, referring to his uncertain status as the son of an attainted traitor; but Warwick points out his descent from Lionel, Duke of Clarence, third son of Edward III. The hostility between Somerset and Plantagenet derives from their respective claims to the throne of England. Both men, vowing to wear their roses as symbols of their eternal hatred, prophesy that blood will be shed over the issue, and Warwick agrees.

⸻⸻⸻⸻

4. **were:** would have been.

7. **Or else:** i.e., they are allowed a choice in expressing agreement with Plantagenet either by saying that he was right or by saying that Somerset was wrong.

15. **mouth:** voice.

17. **bear him:** carry himself.

20. **nice sharp quillets:** fine questions that are difficult to decide.

21. **Good faith:** truly; on my word.

22. **forbearance:** abstaining from commitment.

24. **purblind:** either partially or totally blind.

[Scene IV. London. The Temple Garden.]

Enter Richard Plantagenet, Warwick, Somerset,
Suffolk, and [Vernon and another Lawyer].

Plan. Great lords and gentlemen, what means this
    silence?
Dare no man answer in a case of truth?
    Suf. Within the Temple hall we were too loud:
The garden here is more convenient.   5
    Plan. Then say at once if I maintained the truth;
Or else was wrangling Somerset in the error?
    Suf. Faith, I have been a truant in the law,
And never yet could frame my will to it;
And therefore frame the law unto my will.   10
    Som. Judge you, my lord of Warwick, then, be-
    tween us.
    War. Between two hawks, which flies the higher
    pitch;
Between two dogs, which hath the deeper mouth;   15
Between two blades, which bears the better temper;
Between two horses, which doth bear him best;
Between two girls, which hath the merriest eye—
I have perhaps some shallow spirit of judgment.
But in these nice sharp quillets of the law,   20
Good faith, I am no wiser than a daw.
    Plan. Tut, tut, here is a mannerly forbearance.
The truth appears so naked on my side
That any purblind eye may find it out.

26. **evident:** obvious.

30. **dumb significants:** wordless signs; pantomime.

32. **stands upon:** makes much of; values highly.

38. **colors:** (1) pretexts; (2) personal insignia, hence, choosing of sides; **color:** appearance; trace.

46. **yield:** grant.

48. **subscribe:** submit.

Som. And on my side it is so well appareled,   25
So clear, so shining, and so evident
That it will glimmer through a blind man's eye.
   Plan. Since you are tongue-tied and so loath to
     speak,
In dumb significants proclaim your thoughts.   30
Let him that is a true-born gentleman,
And stands upon the honor of his birth,
If he suppose that I have pleaded truth,
From off this brier pluck a white rose with me.
   Som. Let him that is no coward nor no flatterer,   35
But dare maintain the party of the truth,
Pluck a red rose from off this thorn with me.
   War. I love no colors, and without all color
Of base insinuating flattery
I pluck this white rose with Plantagenet.   40
   Suf. I pluck this red rose with young Somerset,
And say withal I think he held the right.
   Ver. Stay, lords and gentlemen, and pluck no more
Till you conclude that he upon whose side
The fewest roses are cropped from the tree   45
Shall yield the other in the right opinion.
   Som. Good Master Vernon, it is well objected.
If I have fewest, I subscribe in silence.
   Plan. And I.
   Ver. Then for the truth and plainness of the case,   50
I pluck this pale and maiden blossom here,
Giving my verdict on the white rose side.
   Som. Prick not your finger as you pluck it off,
Lest, bleeding, you do paint the white rose red
And fall on my side so, against your will.   55

57. **Opinion shall be surgeon to my hurt:** reputation shall cure me; the idea recalls the proverb "Seek your salve where you got your sore."

67. **counterfeit:** imitate.

72. **that:** i.e., because.

77. **his:** its.

84. **fashion:** i.e., the red rose emblem.

Roses among thorns, symbolizing no pleasure without pain. From Geoffrey Whitney, *A Choice of Emblems* (1586).

Ver. If I, my lord, for my opinion bleed,
Opinion shall be surgeon to my hurt
And keep me on the side where still I am.

  Som. Well, well, come on: who else?

  Law. [*To Somerset*] Unless my study and my books   60
    be false,
The argument you held was wrong in you;
In sign whereof I pluck a white rose too.

  Plan. Now, Somerset, where is your argument?

  Som. Here in my scabbard, meditating that   65
Shall dye your white rose in a bloody red.

  Plan. Meantime your cheeks do counterfeit our
    roses;
For pale they look with fear, as witnessing
The truth on our side.   70

  Som.   No, Plantagenet,
'Tis not for fear but anger, that thy cheeks
Blush for pure shame to counterfeit our roses,
And yet thy tongue will not confess thy error.

  Plan. Hath not thy rose a canker, Somerset?   75

  Som. Hath not thy rose a thorn, Plantagenet?

  Plan. Ay, sharp and piercing, to maintain his truth;
Whiles thy consuming canker eats his falsehood.

  Som. Well, I'll find friends to wear my bleeding
    roses,   80
That shall maintain what I have said is true,
Where false Plantagenet dare not be seen.

  Plan. Now, by this maiden blossom in my hand,
I scorn thee and thy fashion, peevish boy.

  Suf. Turn not thy scorns this way, Plantagenet.   85

90. **grace:** honor.

93. **grandfather:** really, great-grandfather, through his mother, Anne Mortimer.

96. **He bears him on the place's privilege:** i.e., he would not dare to speak so insultingly in precincts less privileged than the garden of the Middle Temple, where he cannot be challenged to defend his words.

102. **attainted:** stained as the heir of a convicted traitor. In such cases, the whole family line was **attainted** and the estate forfeit to the Crown.

103. **exempt from ancient gentry:** debarred from the status of gentry to which his family had long been entitled.

106. **attached, not attainted:** seized, not convicted of treason by due process. Shakespeare has Henry V order the Earl of Cambridge and his confederates arrested and executed on the eve of his departure for France (*Henry V*, Act II, sc. ii). Cambridge's plot to kill the King is well authenticated. The restoration of Plantagenet's inheritance, which Shakespeare dramatizes in Act III, sc. i, of this play, took place in 1426.

110. **partaker:** partisan; ally.

112. **apprehension:** opinion.

114. **still:** ever.

Plan. Proud Pole, I will, and scorn both him and
 thee.
 Suf. I'll turn my part thereof into thy throat.
 Som. Away, away, good William de la Pole!
We grace the yeoman by conversing with him. 90
 War. Now, by God's will, thou wrongst him, Somer-
 set:
His grandfather was Lionel Duke of Clarence,
Third son to the third Edward, King of England.
Spring crestless yeomen from so deep a root? 95
 Plan. He bears him on the place's privilege,
Or durst not, for his craven heart, say thus.
 Som. By Him that made me, I'll maintain my words
On any plot of ground in Christendom.
Was not thy father, Richard Earl of Cambridge, 100
For treason executed in our late King's days?
And, by his treason, standst not thou attainted,
Corrupted, and exempt from ancient gentry?
His trespass yet lives guilty in thy blood;
And, till thou be restored, thou art a yeoman. 105
 Plan. My father was attached, not attainted,
Condemned to die for treason, but no traitor;
And that I'll prove on better men than Somerset,
Were growing time once ripened to my will.
For your partaker Pole and you yourself, 110
I'll note you in my book of memory,
To scourge you for this apprehension.
Look to it well and say you are well warned.
 Som. Ah, thou shalt find us ready for thee still;
And know us by these colors for thy foes, 115
For these my friends in spite of thee shall wear.

118. **cognizance:** badge; symbol.

124. **Have with thee:** I'm with thee; I'm ready when you are.

126. **braved:** challenged; insulted; **perforce:** involuntarily.

128. **object:** put forward.

135. **upon thy party:** in support of your side.

Plan. And, by my soul, this pale and angry rose,
As cognizance of my blood-drinking hate,
Will I forever, and my faction, wear,
Until it wither with me to my grave   120
Or flourish to the height of my degree.

    Suf. Go forward and be choked with thy ambition!
And so farewell until I meet thee next.   *Exit.*

    Som. Have with thee, Pole. Farewell, ambitious
    Richard.   *Exit.* 125

    Plan. How I am braved and must perforce endure
    it!

    War. This blot that they object against your house
Shall be wiped out in the next Parliament
Called for the truce of Winchester and Gloucester;   130
And if thou be not then created York,
I will not live to be accounted Warwick.
Meantime, in signal of my love to thee,
Against proud Somerset and William Pole,
Will I upon thy party wear this rose.   135
And here I prophesy: this brawl today,
Grown to this faction in the Temple garden,
Shall send, between the red rose and the white,
A thousand souls to death and deadly night.

    Plan. Good Master Vernon, I am bound to you,   140
That you on my behalf would pluck a flower.

    Ver. In your behalf still will I wear the same.

    Law. And so will I.

    Plan. Thanks, gentle sir.
Come, let us four to dinner. I dare say   145
This quarrel will drink blood another day.

                               Exeunt.

II.[v.] Plantagenet visits the dying Mortimer in the Tower of London, where Mortimer has been imprisoned for many years because he was a threat to the stability of the house of Lancaster. Mortimer reports that Plantagenet's own father was executed for supporting Mortimer's claim to the throne. Plantagenet's ambition is further enflamed by what Mortimer has told him; if Parliament does not restore his rights, he may seek instead the greater honor to which he is entitled.

||||||||||||||||||||||||||||||||||

5. **pursuivants:** heralds.

6. **Nestor-like:** Nestor was a wise old man who accompanied the Greek party to the siege of Troy. He became an exemplar of both wisdom and antiquity.

9. **exigent:** last extremity; decease.

10. **overborne:** subdued.

16. **witting:** knowing.

17. **nephew:** Shakespeare follows his source in a double confusion by identifying Sir Edmund Mortimer, Owen Glendower's son-in-law, with Edmund Mortimer, 5th Earl of March, and at the same time equating him with another son-in-law of Glendower who was imprisoned in the Tower.

[Scene V. The Tower of London.]

Enter Mortimer, brought in a chair, and Jailers.

Mor. Kind keepers of my weak decaying age,
Let dying Mortimer here rest himself.
Even like a man new haled from the rack,
So fare my limbs with long imprisonment;
And these gray locks, the pursuivants of death,   5
Nestor-like aged in an age of care,
Argue the end of Edmund Mortimer.
These eyes, like lamps whose wasting oil is spent,
Wax dim, as drawing to their exigent;
Weak shoulders overborne with burdening grief,   10
And pithless arms like to a withered vine
That droops his sapless branches to the ground.
Yet are these feet, whose strengthless stay is numb,
Unable to support this lump of clay,
Swift-winged with desire to get a grave,   15
As witting I no other comfort have.
But tell me, keeper, will my nephew come?
Jail. Richard Plantagenet, my lord, will come.
We sent unto the Temple, unto his chamber;
And answer was returned that he will come.   20
Mor. Enough. My soul shall then be satisfied.
Poor gentleman! his wrong doth equal mine.
Since Henry Monmouth first began to reign,
Before whose glory I was great in arms,
This loathsome sequestration have I had;   25

30. **enlargement:** freedom.
36. **late:** recently.
38. **latter:** last.
40. **kindly:** as befits a kinsman.
44. **disease:** trouble.
47. **lavish:** unrestrained.
53. **alliance sake:** sake of our kinship.

And even since then hath Richard been obscured,
Deprived of honor and inheritance.
But now the arbitrator of despairs,
Just Death, kind umpire of men's miseries,
With sweet enlargement doth dismiss me hence.   30
I would his troubles likewise were expired,
That so he might recover what was lost.

Enter Richard [Plantagenet].

   Jail. My lord, your loving nephew now is come.
   Mor. Richard Plantagenet, my friend, is he come?
   Plan. Ay, noble uncle, thus ignobly used,   35
Your nephew, late despised Richard, comes.
   Mor. Direct mine arms I may embrace his neck,
And in his bosom spend my latter gasp.
Oh, tell me when my lips do touch his cheeks,
That I may kindly give one fainting kiss.   40
And now declare, sweet stem from York's great stock,
Why didst thou say of late thou wert despised?
   Plan. First, lean thine aged back against mine arm;
And, in that ease, I'll tell thee my disease.
This day, in argument upon a case,   45
Some words there grew 'twixt Somerset and me;
Among which terms he used his lavish tongue
And did upbraid me with my father's death:
Which obloquy set bars before my tongue,
Else with the like I had requited him.   50
Therefore, good uncle, for my father's sake,
In honor of a true Plantagenet
And for alliance sake, declare the cause

59. **Discover:** reveal.

64. **Richard:** Richard II, son of Edward, the Black Prince.

67. **whose:** i.e., that of Henry IV, the first Lancastrian King.

74. **mother:** Philippa of Hainaut, who married Edmund Mortimer, third Earl of March; she was thus grandmother of the fifth Earl.

79. **haughty:** aspiring.

My father, Earl of Cambridge, lost his head.

　Mor. That cause, fair nephew, that imprisoned me　　55
And hath detained me all my flow'ring youth
Within a loathsome dungeon, there to pine,
Was cursed instrument of his decease.

　Plan. Discover more at large what cause that was,
For I am ignorant and cannot guess.　　60

　Mor. I will, if that my fading breath permit,
And death approach not ere my tale be done.
Henry the Fourth, grandfather to this king,
Deposed his nephew Richard, Edward's son,
The first-begotten and the lawful heir　　65
Of Edward, King, the third of that descent;
During whose reign the Percies of the North,
Finding his usurpation most unjust,
Endeavored my advancement to the throne.
The reason moved these warlike lords to this　　70
Was for that—young King Richard thus removed,
Leaving no heir begotten of his body—
I was the next by birth and parentage;
For by my mother I derived am
From Lionel Duke of Clarence, the third son　　75
To King Edward the Third; whereas he
From John of Gaunt doth bring his pedigree,
Being but fourth of that heroic line.
But mark: as in this haughty great attempt
They labored to plant the rightful heir,　　80
I lost my liberty and they their lives.
Long after this, when Henry the Fifth,
Succeeding his father Bolingbroke, did reign,
Thy father, Earl of Cambridge, then derived

85. **Edmund Langley:** i.e., Edmund of Langley. Plantagenet derived from him his claim to the duchy of York and another claim to the throne.

88. **weening:** thinking.

89. **diadem:** sovereign crown. Edmund Mortimer, 5th Earl of March, seems actually to have revealed Cambridge's plot to Henry V.

108. **redeem the passage of your age:** i.e., gain him a few more years of life.

From famous Edmund Langley, Duke of York,   85
Marrying my sister, that thy mother was,
Again in pity of my hard distress
Levied an army, weening to redeem
And have installed me in the diadem;
But, as the rest, so fell that noble earl   90
And was beheaded. Thus the Mortimers,
In whom the title rested, were suppressed.

    Plan. Of which, my lord, your Honor is the last.

    Mor. True, and thou seest that I no issue have,
And that my fainting words do warrant death.   95
Thou art my heir: the rest I wish thee gather;
But yet be wary in thy studious care.

    Plan. Thy grave admonishments prevail with me:
But yet, methinks, my father's execution
Was nothing less than bloody tyranny.   100

    Mor. With silence, nephew, be thou politic.
Strong-fixed is the house of Lancaster
And, like a mountain, not to be removed.
But now thy uncle is removing hence,
As princes do their courts when they are cloyed   105
With long continuance in a settled place.

    Plan. O uncle, would some part of my young years
Might but redeem the passage of your age!

    Mor. Thou dost then wrong me, as that slaughterer
      doth   110
Which giveth many wounds when one will kill.
Mourn not, except thou sorrow for my good;
Only give order for my funeral.
And so farewell, and fair be all thy hopes,
And prosperous be thy life in peace and war!   *Dies.* 115

117. **pilgrimage:** normal term of human life.

118. **overpassed:** spent.

120. **let that rest:** i.e., that remains to be revealed; I will keep it to myself.

123. **dusky:** dim; long kept from burning brightly.

125. **for:** as for.

130. **make my ill the advantage of my good:** make the injustice my excuse for pressing my claim to the crown by force. Henry IV seized the crown under similar circumstances.

Plan. And peace, no war, befall thy parting soul!
In prison hast thou spent a pilgrimage,
And like a hermit overpassed thy days.
Well, I will lock his counsel in my breast;
And what I do imagine let that rest.   120
Keepers, convey him hence, and I myself
Will see his burial better than his life.
   [*Exeunt Jailers, bearing out the body of Mortimer.*]
Here dies the dusky torch of Mortimer,
Choked with ambition of the meaner sort.
And for those wrongs, those bitter injuries,   125
Which Somerset hath offered to my house,
I doubt not but with honor to redress;
And therefore haste I to the Parliament,
Either to be restored to my blood,
Or make my ill the advantage of my good.   130
                               Exit.

THE FIRST PART
OF
HENRY THE SIXTH

ACT III

III.i. King Henry has convened Parliament, and at the outset Gloucester and Winchester exchange bitter accusations. The assembly is further disturbed by the entrance of the Mayor, followed by men of the parties of Gloucester and Winchester, who have been fighting with stones in the streets. The King orders the fighting to cease and finally persuades Gloucester and Winchester to make a show of patching up their quarrel. Warwick petitions for the restoration of Richard Plantagenet's rights. The King agrees and in addition creates him Duke of York. In the manner of a Chorus, the Duke of Exeter, Winchester's brother, prophesies that the truce will not last; he foresees the fulfillment of the prophecy that Henry born at Monmouth (Henry V) would win all but Henry born at Windsor (Henry VI) would lose all.

Ent. **put up:** present.

5. **without invention, suddenly:** extemporaneously, without contriving arguments in advance.

11. **preferred:** brought up.

14. **rehearse:** recite in exact detail; **method:** orderly exposition.

16. **lewd:** wicked; **pestiferous:** destructive.

ACT III

Scene I. [London. The Parliament House.]

Flourish. Enter King, Exeter, Gloucester, Winchester, Warwick, Somerset, Suffolk, Richard Plantagenet, [and others]. Gloucester offers to put up a bill; Winchester snatches it, tears it.

Win. Comest thou with deep premeditated lines,
With written pamphlets studiously devised,
Humphrey of Gloucester? If thou canst accuse,
Or aught intendst to lay unto my charge,
Do it without invention, suddenly;   5
As I with sudden and extemporal speech
Purpose to answer what thou canst object.
   Glou. Presumptuous priest! this place commands
     my patience,
Or thou shouldst find thou hast dishonored me.   10
Think not, although in writing I preferred
The manner of thy vile outrageous crimes,
That therefore I have forged, or am not able
Verbatim to rehearse the method of my pen.
No, prelate, such is thy audacious wickedness,   15
Thy lewd, pestiferous, and dissentious pranks,

46

18. **pernicious:** wicked; **usurer:** one who lends money at exorbitant rates of interest.

19. **Froward:** perverse.

20. **beseems:** becomes.

27. **envious:** hostile; **swelling:** resentful.

28. **vouchsafe:** condescend.

34. **preferreth:** advances; promotes.

38. **because:** in order that; **sway:** rule.

44. **bastard:** John of Gaunt's mistress, Catherine Swynford, gave birth to Henry Beaufort, a surname later bestowed on her offspring by Gaunt, before they were married. Gaunt eventually had the Beauforts declared legitimate.

As very infants prattle of thy pride!
Thou art a most pernicious usurer,
Froward by nature, enemy to peace;
Lascivious, wanton, more than well beseems   20
A man of thy profession and degree;
And for thy treachery, what's more manifest?
In that thou laidst a trap to take my life,
As well at London Bridge as at the Tower.
Beside, I fear me, if thy thoughts were sifted,   25
The King, thy sovereign, is not quite exempt
From envious malice of thy swelling heart.

   Win. Gloucester, I do defy thee. Lords, vouchsafe
To give me hearing what I shall reply.
If I were covetous, ambitious, or perverse,   30
As he will have me, how am I so poor?
Or how haps it I seek not to advance
Or raise myself, but keep my wonted calling?
And for dissension, who preferreth peace
More than I do?—except I be provoked.   35
No, my good lords, it is not that offends;
It is not that that hath incensed the Duke.
It is because no one should sway but he;
No one but he should be about the King;
And that engenders thunder in his breast   40
And makes him roar these accusations forth.
But he shall know I am as good—

   Glou.   As good!
Thou bastard of my grandfather!

   Win. Ay, lordly sir; for what are you, I pray,   45
But one imperious in another's throne?

   Glou. Am I not Protector, saucy priest?

49. **keeps:** safeguards himself.

50. **patronage:** protect.

52. **reverent:** worthy of respect.

58. **my lord:** Gloucester; **religious:** pious.

59. **office that belongs to such:** i.e., the duty of respect owed to religious men like Winchester.

60. **His Lordship:** Winchester.

67. **sirrah:** a term used to men of base birth, referring bitterly to the questionable state of his inheritance.

68. **verdict:** judgment.

71. **weal:** welfare; commonwealth.

Win. And am not I a prelate of the church?

Glou. Yes, as an outlaw in a castle keeps

And useth it to patronage his theft.   50

Win. Unreverent Gloucester!

Glou.   Thou art reverent

Touching thy spiritual function, not thy life.

Win. Rome shall remedy this.

War.   Roam thither, then.   55

Som. My lord, it were your duty to forbear.

War. Ay, see the Bishop be not overborne.

Som. Methinks my lord should be religious

And know the office that belongs to such.

War. Methinks His Lordship should be humbler: 60

It fitteth not a prelate so to plead.

Som. Yes, when his holy state is touched so near.

War. State holy or unhallowed, what of that?

Is not His Grace Protector to the King?

Plan. [*Aside*] Plantagenet, I see, must hold his   65
        tongue,

Lest it be said, "Speak, sirrah, when you should.

Must your bold verdict enter talk with lords?"

Else would I have a fling at Winchester.

King. Uncles of Gloucester and of Winchester,   70

The special watchmen of our English weal,

I would prevail, if prayers might prevail,

To join your hearts in love and amity.

Oh, what a scandal is it to our crown

That two such noble peers as ye should jar!   75

Believe me, lords, my tender years can tell

Civil dissension is a viperous worm

100. **peevish:** childish.

That gnaws the bowels of the commonwealth.
   A noise within, "Down with the tawny coats!"
What tumult's this?   80
 War.   An uproar, I dare warrant,
Begun through malice of the Bishop's men.
      A noise again, "Stones! stones!"

    Enter Mayor, [attended].

 May. O, my good lords, and virtuous Henry,
Pity the City of London, pity us!   85
The Bishop and the Duke of Gloucester's men,
Forbidden late to carry any weapon,
Have filled their pockets full of pebble stones
And, banding themselves in contrary parts,
Do pelt so fast at one another's pate   90
That many have their giddy brains knocked out.
Our windows are broke down in every street
And we for fear compelled to shut our shops.

Enter [Servingmen,] in skirmish, with bloody pates.

 King. We charge you, on allegiance to ourself,
To hold your slaught'ring hands and keep the peace.   95
Pray, uncle Gloucester, mitigate this strife.
 1. Ser. Nay, if we be forbidden stones, we'll fall to it
with our teeth.
 2. Ser. Do what ye dare, we are as resolute.
        Skirmish again.
 Glou. You of my household, leave this peevish broil   100
And set this unaccustomed fight aside.

105. **prince:** ruler.

107. **inkhorn mate:** bookish fellow (Winchester, who, as a prelate, could be assumed to be scholarly).

111. **pitch a field:** furnish or prepare a battlefield.

113. **And if:** if.

119. **study:** endeavor.

128. **stoop:** submit.

3. Ser. My lord, we know your Grace to be a man
Just and upright; and, for your royal birth,
Inferior to none but to His Majesty;
And ere that we will suffer such a prince,   105
So kind a father of the commonweal,
To be disgraced by an inkhorn mate,
We and our wives and children all will fight
And have our bodies slaughtered by thy foes.

   1. Ser. Ay, and the very parings of our nails   110
Shall pitch a field when we are dead.   *Begin again.*
   Glou.   Stay, stay, I say!
And if you love me, as you say you do,
Let me persuade you to forbear awhile.

   King. Oh, how this discord doth afflict my soul!   115
Can you, my lord of Winchester, behold
My sighs and tears and will not once relent?
Who should be pitiful, if you be not?
Or who should study to prefer a peace,
If holy churchmen take delight in broils?   120

   War. Yield, my Lord Protector! Yield, Winchester!
Except you mean with obstinate repulse
To slay your sovereign and destroy the realm.
You see what mischief and what murder too
Hath been enacted through your enmity: 125
Then be at peace, except ye thirst for blood.

   Win. He shall submit, or I will never yield.

   Glou. Compassion on the King commands me stoop,
Or I would see his heart out, ere the priest
Should ever get that privilege of me.   130

   War. Behold, my lord of Winchester, the Duke

140-41. **kindly gird:** rebuke appropriate to a man of religious profession.

157. **Content:** agreed.

159. **physic:** medicine.

Hath banished moody discontented fury,
As by his smoothed brows it doth appear.
Why look you still so stern and tragical?

   Glou. Here, Winchester, I offer thee my hand.   135

   King. Fie, uncle Beaufort! I have heard you preach
That malice was a great and grievous sin;
And will not you maintain the thing you teach,
But prove a chief offender in the same?

   War. [*Aside*] Sweet King! the Bishop hath a kindly 140
      gird.—
For shame, my lord of Winchester, relent!
What, shall a child instruct you what to do?

   Win. Well, Duke of Gloucester, I will yield to thee:
Love for thy love and hand for hand I give.   145

   Glou. [*Aside*] Ay, but, I fear me, with a hollow
      heart.—
See here, my friends and loving countrymen:
This token serveth for a flag of truce
Betwixt ourselves and all our followers.   150
So help me God, as I dissemble not!

   Win. [*Aside*] So help me God, as I intend it not!

   King. O loving uncle, kind Duke of Gloucester,
How joyful am I made by this contract!
Away, my masters! Trouble us no more;   155
But join in friendship, as your lords have done.

   1. Ser. Content. I'll to the surgeon's.

   2. Ser.   And so will I.

   3. Ser. And I will see what physic the tavern
affords.   *Exeunt* [*Servingmen, Mayor, etc.*]. 160

   War. Accept this scroll, most gracious sovereign,

163. **exhibit:** present for consideration.

164. **urged:** mentioned; offered.

168-69. **occasions/ At Eltham Place I told your Majesty:** i.e., reasons related to the King at Eltham Place, one of the royal residences.

172. **restored to his blood:** repossessed of his lineage and the inheritance belonging to it.

183. **reguerdon:** reward.

189. **grudge one thought:** think one hostile thought.

Which in the right of Richard Plantagenet
We do exhibit to your Majesty.

   Glou. Well urged, my Lord of Warwick: for, sweet
     prince,   165
And if your Grace mark every circumstance,
You have great reason to do Richard right;
Especially for those occasions
At Eltham Place I told your Majesty.

   King. And those occasions, uncle, were of force.   170
Therefore, my loving lords, our pleasure is
That Richard be restored to his blood.

   War. Let Richard be restored to his blood;
So shall his father's wrongs be recompensed.

   Win. As will the rest, so willeth Winchester.   175

   King. If Richard will be true, not that alone
But all the whole inheritance I give
That doth belong unto the house of York,
From whence you spring by lineal descent.

   Plan. Thy humble servant vows obedience   180
And humble service till the point of death.

   King. Stoop then and set your knee against my foot;
And, in reguerdon of that duty done,
I gird thee with the valiant sword of York.
Rise, Richard, like a true Plantagenet,   185
And rise created princely Duke of York.

   Plan. And so thrive Richard as thy foes may fall!
And as my duty springs, so perish they
That grudge one thought against your Majesty!

   All. Welcome, high prince, the mighty Duke of 190
     York!

198. **disanimates:** dispirits.

211. **prophecy:** Edward Hall, in *The Union of the Two Noble and Illustrious Families of Lancaster and York*, attributed a similar prophecy to Henry V himself when it was reported to him that a son had been born to him at Windsor.

   Som. [*Aside*] Perish, base prince, ignoble Duke of
     York!
   Glou. Now will it best avail your Majesty
To cross the seas and to be crowned in France.   195
The presence of a king engenders love
Amongst his subjects and his loyal friends,
As it disanimates his enemies.
   King. When Gloucester says the word, King Henry
     goes;   200
For friendly counsel cuts off many foes.
   Glou. Your ships already are in readiness.
          Sennet. Flourish. Exeunt. Manet Exeter.
   Exe. Ay, we may march in England or in France,
Not seeing what is likely to ensue.
This late dissension grown betwixt the peers   205
Burns under feigned ashes of forged love,
And will at last break out into a flame.
As festered members rot but by degree,
Till bones and flesh and sinews fall away,
So will this base and envious discord breed.   210
And now I fear that fatal prophecy
Which in the time of Henry named the Fifth
Was in the mouth of every sucking babe:
That Henry born at Monmouth should win all
And Henry born at Windsor should lose all: 215
Which is so plain that Exeter doth wish
His days may finish ere that hapless time.

                     Exit.

III.ii. La Pucelle and the Dauphin's followers capture Rouen by a trick. Talbot, Burgundy, and Bedford resolve to retake the city or die in the attempt. The feeble old Bedford watches from a chair outside the city walls. Sir John Fastolfe again plays the coward, but Bedford's patience is rewarded by the sight of the rout of the French and he dies content. Talbot plans to consolidate their position in Rouen and then go on to Paris for the coronation of the young King. He orders the proper funeral rites for the Duke of Bedford.

▬▬▬▬▬▬▬▬▬▬▬▬▬▬▬▬▬▬▬▬

2. **policy:** craft; stratagem.

10. **mean:** means.

16. **the market bell is rung:** the ringing of the bell signified the beginning of the day's business in the market.

Scene II. [France. Before Rouen.]

Enter La Pucelle, disguised, with four Soldiers, with
sacks upon their backs.

Puc. These are the city gates, the gates of Rouen,
Through which our policy must make a breach.
Take heed, be wary how you place your words:
Talk like the vulgar sort of market men
That come to gather money for their corn.   5
If we have entrance, as I hope we shall,
And that we find the slothful watch but weak,
I'll by a sign give notice to our friends,
That Charles the Dauphin may encounter them.
Sol. Our sacks shall be a mean to sack the city,   10
And we be lords and rulers over Rouen:
Therefore we'll knock.   *Knocks.*
Watch. [*Within*] *Qui est là?*
Puc. Paysans, pauvres gens de France.
Poor market folks that come to sell their corn.   15
Watch. Enter, go in: the market bell is rung.
Puc. Now, Rouen, I'll shake thy bulwarks to the
    ground.   *Exeunt.*

Enter Charles, Bastard, Alençon, [Reignier, and
forces].

Char. St. Denis bless this happy stratagem!
And once again we'll sleep secure in Rouen.   20

21. **practisants:** partners in trickery.

26. **No way to that, for weakness, which she entered:** no other entrance to the city compares in weakness with the one which she entered.

29. **Talbonites:** Talbot and his followers.

32. **shine it:** let it shine.

34. **delays have dangerous ends:** proverbial.

35. **presently:** at once.

Ent. 36. **in an excursion:** engaged in skirmishing.

41. **unawares:** when we were unaware.

42. **pride:** power that would take pride in our capture.

View of Rouen. From John Speed. *A Prospect of the Most Famous Parts of the World* (1632).

Bas. Here entered Pucelle and her practisants.
Now she is there, how will she specify
Where is the best and safest passage in?

Reign. By thrusting out a torch from yonder tower,
Which, once discerned, shows that her meaning is,   25
No way to that, for weakness, which she entered.

*Enter La Pucelle on the top, thrusting out a torch
burning.*

Puc. Behold, this is the happy wedding torch
That joineth Rouen unto her countrymen,
But burning fatal to the Talbonites!   [*Exit.*]

Bas. See, noble Charles, the beacon of our friend;   30
The burning torch in yonder turret stands.

Char. Now shine it like a comet of revenge,
A prophet to the fall of all our foes!

Reign. Defer no time, delays have dangerous ends:
Enter, and cry "The Dauphin!" presently   35
And then do execution on the watch.   *Alarum.*
        [*Exeunt.*]

An alarum. [Enter] Talbot in an excursion.

Tal. France, thou shalt rue this treason with thy
        tears,
If Talbot but survive thy treachery.
Pucelle, that witch, that damned sorceress,   40
Hath wrought this hellish mischief unawares,
That hardly we escaped the pride of France.   *Exit.*

47. **darnel:** a common weed.
58. **of all despite:** completely made up of malice.

John, Duke of Bedford. Engraving by Silvester Harding, after a manuscript original.

*An alarum: excursions. Bedford, brought in sick in a
chair. Enter Talbot and Burgundy without: within La
Pucelle, Charles, Bastard, [Alençon,] and Reignier, on
the walls.*

Puc. Good morrow, gallants! want ye corn for
    bread?
I think the Duke of Burgundy will fast   45
Before he'll buy again at such a rate.
'Twas full of darnel. Do you like the taste?
    Bur. Scoff on, vile fiend and shameless courtesan!
I trust ere long to choke thee with thine own,
And make thee curse the harvest of that corn.   50
    Char. Your Grace may starve perhaps before that
    time.
    Bed. Oh, let no words, but deeds, revenge this
    treason!
    Puc. What will you do, good graybeard? Break a   55
    lance,
And run a tilt at Death within a chair?
    Tal. Foul fiend of France, and hag of all despite,
Encompassed with thy lustful paramours!
Becomes it thee to taunt his valiant age   60
And twit with cowardice a man half dead?
Damsel, I'll have a bout with you again,
Or else let Talbot perish with this shame.
    Puc. Are ye so hot, sir? Yet, Pucelle, hold thy peace:
If Talbot do but thunder, rain will follow.   65
           [The English] whisper together in council.

68. **Belike:** perhaps.

69. **try:** test; **if that:** whether.

70. **railing:** scolding; **Hecate:** the Greek goddess who controlled the activities of witches; hence, a witch.

75. **keep:** keep to for safety.

79. **God b'uy:** God be with you; good-by.

95. **crazy:** frail of body; feeble.

God speed the parliament! Who shall be the speaker?

    Tal. Dare ye come forth and meet us in the field?

    Puc. Belike your Lordship takes us then for fools,

To try if that our own be ours or no.

    Tal. I speak not to that railing Hecate,   70

But unto thee, Alençon, and the rest:

Will ye, like soldiers, come and fight it out?

    Alen. Signior, no.

    Tal. Signior, hang! Base muleters of France!

Like peasant footboys do they keep the walls,   75

And dare not take up arms like gentlemen.

    Puc. Away, captains! Let's get us from the walls;

For Talbot means no goodness by his looks.

God b'uy, my lord! We came but to tell you

That we are here.   *Exeunt from the walls.*   80

    Tal. And there will we be too, ere it be long,

Or else reproach be Talbot's greatest fame!

Vow, Burgundy, by honor of thy house,

Pricked on by public wrongs sustained in France,

Either to get the town again or die.   85

And I, as sure as English Henry lives

And as his father here was conqueror,

As sure as in this late-betrayed town

Great Coeur de Lion's heart was buried,

So sure I swear to get the town or die.   90

    Bur. My vows are equal partners with thy vows.

    Tal. But, ere we go, regard this dying prince,

The valiant Duke of Bedford. Come, my lord,

We will bestow you in some better place,

Fitter for sickness and for crazy age.   95

    Bed. Lord Talbot, do not so dishonor me.

101. **stout:** valiant; **Pendragon:** Uther Pendragon, father of the renowned King Arthur.

104. **as myself:** instilled with the same spirit as I displayed.

108. **out of hand:** without delay.

113. **like:** likely.

Here will I sit, before the walls of Rouen,
And will be partner of your weal or woe.

   Bur. Courageous Bedford, let us now persuade you.

   Bed. Not to be gone from hence; for once I read   100
That stout Pendragon in his litter sick
Came to the field and vanquished his foes.
Methinks I should revive the soldiers' hearts,
Because I ever found them as myself.

   Tal. Undaunted spirit in a dying breast!   105
Then be it so. Heavens keep old Bedford safe!
And now no more ado, brave Burgundy,
But gather we our forces out of hand
And set upon our boasting enemy.

       Exeunt [all but Bedford and Attendants].

*An alarum: excursions. Enter Sir John Fastolfe and a
Captain.*

   Capt. Whither away, Sir John Fastolfe, in such 110
    haste?

   Fas. Whither away! to save myself by flight.
We are like to have the overthrow again.

   Capt. What! will you fly, and leave Lord Talbot?

   Fas.   Ay, 115
All the Talbots in the world, to save my life.   *Exit.*

   Capt. Cowardly knight! ill fortune follow thee! *Exit.*

*Retreat: excursions. La Pucelle, Alençon, and Charles
                            fly.*

   Bed. Now, quiet soul, depart when Heaven please,
For I have seen our enemies' overthrow.
What is the trust or strength of foolish man?   120

122. **glad and fain:** i.e., forced to flee and glad to be able to do so.

129. **gentle:** courteous.

131. **old familiar:** habitual demon attendant, such as were supposed to help witches in their sorcery.

132. **braves:** taunts.

132-33. **Charles his gleeks:** Charles's scoffs.

134. **amort:** spiritless.

136. **take some order:** plan orderly arrangements.

143. **exequies:** funeral rites.

144. **couched:** leveled in attack.

145. **sway:** rule.

They that of late were daring with their scoffs
Are glad and fain by flight to save themselves.

Bedford dies, and is carried in by two in his chair.

An alarum. Enter Talbot, Burgundy, and the rest.

   Tal. Lost and recovered in a day again!
This is a double honor, Burgundy.
Yet Heavens have glory for this victory!   125
   Bur. Warlike and martial Talbot, Burgundy
Enshrines thee in his heart and there erects
Thy noble deeds as valor's monuments.
   Tal. Thanks, gentle Duke. But where is Pucelle
     now?   130
I think her old familiar is asleep.
Now where's the Bastard's braves and Charles his
     gleeks?
What, all amort? Rouen hangs her head for grief
That such a valiant company are fled.   135
Now will we take some order in the town,
Placing therein some expert officers,
And then depart to Paris to the King,
For there young Henry with his nobles lie.
   Bur. What wills Lord Talbot pleaseth Burgundy.   140
   Tal. But yet, before we go, let's not forget
The noble Duke of Bedford late deceased,
But see his exequies fulfilled in Rouen.
A braver soldier never couched lance,
A gentler heart did never sway in court;   145
But kings and mightiest potentates must die,
For that's the end of human misery.

                            Exeunt.

III.iii. La Pucelle, undismayed at the loss of Rouen, proposes that the French entice the Duke of Burgundy to abandon the English. An opportunity occurs when Burgundy and his forces appear at a sufficient distance from Talbot to make possible a parley. Burgundy is won by La Pucelle's persuasive words to renew his allegiance to France.

⁂

3. **Care is no cure:** proverbial; **corrosive:** i.e., an aggravation.

8. **be but ruled:** i.e., take her advice.

10. **diffidence:** distrust.

24. **extirped:** rooted out.

26. **title of:** legal right to.

Scene III. [The plains near Rouen.]

Enter Charles, Bastard, Alençon, La Pucelle, [and forces].

Puc. Dismay not, princes, at this accident,
Nor grieve that Rouen is so recovered.
Care is no cure, but rather corrosive,
For things that are not to be remedied.
Let frantic Talbot triumph for a while   5
And like a peacock sweep along his tail;
We'll pull his plumes and take away his train,
If Dauphin and the rest will be but ruled.
   Char. We have been guided by thee hitherto
And of thy cunning had no diffidence;   10
One sudden foil shall never breed distrust.
   Bas. Search out thy wit for secret policies,
And we will make thee famous through the world.
   Alen. We'll set thy statue in some holy place
And have thee reverenced like a blessed saint.   15
Employ thee then, sweet virgin, for our good.
   Puc. Then thus it must be; this doth Joan devise:
By fair persuasions mixed with sugared words
We will entice the Duke of Burgundy
To leave the Talbot and to follow us.   20
   Char. Ay, marry, sweeting, if we could do that,
France were no place for Henry's warriors;
Nor should that nation boast it so with us,
But be extirped from our provinces.
   Alen. Forever should they be expulsed from France,   25
And not have title of an earldom here.

34. **in favor:** as a favor to the French, since it gives them opportunity to speak to him.

Martial drummers. From Geoffrey Whitney, *A Choice of Emblems* (1586).

Puc. Your Honors shall perceive how I will work
To bring this matter to the wished end.
                              Drum sounds afar off.
Hark! by the sound of drum you may perceive
Their powers are marching unto Paris-ward.   30

*Here sound an English march. [Enter, and pass over
      at a distance, Talbot and his forces.]*

There goes the Talbot, with his colors spread,
And all the troops of English after him.

*French march. [Enter the Duke of Burgundy and
                  forces.]*

Now in the rearward comes the Duke and his.
Fortune in favor makes him lag behind.
Summon a parley: we will talk with him.   35
                              Trumpets sound a parley.
  Char. A parley with the Duke of Burgundy!
  Bur. Who craves a parley with the Burgundy?
  Puc. The princely Charles of France, thy country-
    man.
  Bur. What sayst thou, Charles? for I am marching   40
    hence.
  Char. Speak, Pucelle, and enchant him with thy
    words.
  Puc. Brave Burgundy, undoubted hope of France!
Stay, let thy humble handmaid speak to thee.   45
  Bur. Speak on; but be not overtedious.
  Puc. Look on thy country, look on fertile France,

51. **tender-dying:** dying at a tender age.

60. **stained spots:** spots that stain; disgraces.

64. **exclaims on:** denounces.

66. **birth and lawful progeny:** legitimacy of birth.

72. **fugitive:** renegade; one not to be trusted, as a traitor to his own country.

74. **the Duke of Orléans:** Shakespeare ignores actual historical chronology here: Joan of Arc was dead by the time Burgundy changed his allegiance from the English to the French king in 1435. Charles, Duke of Orléans, who had been a prisoner in England since the Battle of Agincourt (1415), was not released until 1440, partly as a consequence of Burgundy's defection.

And see the cities and the towns defaced
By wasting ruin of the cruel foe.
As looks the mother on her lowly babe   50
When death doth close his tender-dying eyes,
See, see the pining malady of France;
Behold the wounds, the most unnatural wounds,
Which thou thyself hast given her woeful breast.
Oh, turn thy edged sword another way;   55
Strike those that hurt, and hurt not those that help.
One drop of blood drawn from thy country's bosom
Should grieve thee more than streams of foreign gore.
Return thee therefore with a flood of tears,
And wash away thy country's stained spots.   60
   Bur. [*Aside*] Either she hath bewitched me with
    her words,
Or nature makes me suddenly relent.
   Puc. Besides, all French and France exclaims on
    thee,   65
Doubting thy birth and lawful progeny.
Who joinst thou with but with a lordly nation
That will not trust thee but for profit's sake?
When Talbot hath set footing once in France
And fashioned thee that instrument of ill,   70
Who then but English Henry will be lord,
And thou be thrust out like a fugitive?
Call we to mind, and mark but this for proof,
Was not the Duke of Orléans thy foe?
And was he not in England prisoner?   75
But when they heard he was thine enemy,
They set him free, without his ransom paid,
In spite of Burgundy and all his friends.

94. **fresh:** strengthened.
96. **bravely:** splendidly.
99. **prejudice:** damage.

Philip, Duke of Burgundy. From Pompilio Totti, *Ritratti et elogii di capitani illustri* (1635).

See, then, thou fightst against thy countrymen
And joinst with them will be thy slaughter-men.   80
Come, come, return! Return, thou wandering lord:
Charles and the rest will take thee in their arms.

   Bur. [*Aside*] I am vanquished; these haughty
     words of hers
Have battered me like roaring cannon shot   85
And made me almost yield upon my knees.—
Forgive me, country and sweet countrymen,
And, lords, accept this hearty kind embrace.
My forces and my power of men are yours.
So farewell, Talbot: I'll no longer trust thee.   90

   Puc. Done like a Frenchman: [*Aside*] turn, and
     turn again!

   Char. Welcome, brave Duke! Thy friendship makes
     us fresh.

   Bas. And doth beget new courage in our breasts.   95

   Alen. Pucelle hath bravely played her part in this
And doth deserve a coronet of gold.

   Char. Now let us on, my lords, and join our powers,
And seek how we may prejudice the foe.

                         Exeunt.

III.iv. Talbot presents his respects to King Henry, who creates him Earl of Shrewsbury. While they proceed to the place of coronation, followers of Somerset and Plantagenet come to blows over their respective loyalties and agree to ask the King for permission to fight it out.

⁜⁜⁜⁜⁜⁜⁜⁜⁜⁜⁜⁜⁜⁜⁜⁜⁜⁜⁜⁜⁜⁜⁜⁜⁜⁜

4. **duty:** homage as a subject.
17. **as yet:** although.

View of Paris. From John Speed, *A Prospect of the Most Famous Parts of the World* (1632).

Scene IV. [Paris. The palace.]

Enter the King, Gloucester, Winchester, York, Suffolk,
Somerset, Warwick, Exeter, [Vernon, Basset, and
others]: to them with his Soldiers, Talbot.

  Tal. My gracious prince and honorable peers,
Hearing of your arrival in this realm,
I have awhile given truce unto my wars,
To do my duty to my sovereign:
In sign whereof, this arm, that hath reclaimed   5
To your obedience fifty fortresses,
Twelve cities, and seven walled towns of strength,
Beside five hundred prisoners of esteem,
Lets fall his sword before your Highness' feet,
And with submissive loyalty of heart   10
Ascribes the glory of his conquest got
First to my God and next unto your Grace. [*Kneels.*]
  King. Is this the Lord Talbot, uncle Gloucester,
That hath so long been resident in France?
  Glou. Yes, if it please your Majesty, my Liege.   15
  King. Welcome, brave captain and victorious lord!
When I was young—as yet I am not old—
I do remember how my father said
A stouter champion never handled sword.
Long since we were resolved of your truth,   20
Your faithful service, and your toil in war;
Yet never have you tasted our reward,
Or been reguerdoned with so much as thanks,
Because till now we never saw your face.

32. **patronage:** defend.

38. **law of arms:** the prohibition against personal fights in a royal precinct.

39. **present:** immediate.

40. **broach:** tap (like a cask of liquor); **dearest:** most vital.

41. **crave:** request.

44. **miscreant:** coward.

45. **would:** would wish.

Therefore, stand up; and, for these good deserts,   25
We here create you Earl of Shrewsbury;
And in our coronation take your place.
Sennet. Flourish. Exeunt [all but Vernon and Basset].
    Ver. Now, sir, to you, that were so hot at sea,
Disgracing of these colors that I wear
In honor of my noble Lord of York: 30
Darest thou maintain the former words thou spakest?
    Bass. Yes, sir; as well as you dare patronage
The envious barking of your saucy tongue
Against my lord the Duke of Somerset.
    Ver. Sirrah, thy lord I honor as he is.   35
    Bass. Why, what is he? As good a man as York.
    Ver. Hark ye, not so! In witness, take ye that.
                                        Strikes him.
    Bass. Villain, thou knowest the law of arms is such
That whoso draws a sword, 'tis present death,
Or else this blow should broach thy dearest blood.   40
But I'll unto His Majesty and crave
I may have liberty to venge this wrong;
When thou shalt see I'll meet thee to thy cost.
    Ver. Well, miscreant, I'll be there as soon as you;
And, after, meet you sooner than you would.   45
                                        Exeunt.

THE FIRST PART
OF
HENRY THE SIXTH

ACT IV

IV.i. Henry VI is crowned. When Fastolfe appears with a letter from Burgundy, Talbot charges him with cowardice, removes the Garter emblem from his leg, and tells how Fastolfe deserted him at Patay and thus lost the battle. Burgundy's letter reports his defection; Talbot leaves, determined to make Burgundy regret it. Vernon and Basset, belligerent followers of Somerset and Plantagenet, report their cause to the King, who is distressed at this renewed outbreak of faction. The King orders the men to forget their quarrel and attempts to smooth things over by putting on a red rose, saying that it does not signify greater love to Somerset than to York, since both are his kinsmen. He appoints York to be Regent of France, replacing the deceased Bedford, and appoints Somerset to join his horse with York's foot soldiers. York is uneasy at the King's adoption of the red rose, but Warwick tries to convince him that it was a meaningless fancy and York controls his feelings. Exeter again states the moral of the scene: it's bad enough when a child rules; but it's far worse when malicious rivalry destroys the unity of the kingdom.

〰〰〰〰〰〰〰〰〰〰〰

4. **elect:** choose.
6. **pretend:** intend.

ACT IV

Scene I. [Paris. A hall of state.]

Enter King, Gloucester, Winchester, York, Suffolk, Somerset, Warwick, Talbot, Exeter, [the] Governor [of Paris, and others].

Glou. Lord Bishop, set the crown upon his head.
Win. God save King Henry, of that name the Sixth!
Glou. Now, Governor of Paris, take your oath,
                              [*Governor kneels.*]
That you elect no other King but him;
Esteem none friends but such as are his friends,   5
And none your foes but such as shall pretend
Malicious practices against his state:
This shall ye do, so help you righteous God!
                              [*Governor rises and exit.*]

Enter [Sir John] Fastolfe.

Fas. My gracious sovereign, as I rode from Calais,
To haste unto your coronation,   10
A letter was delivered to my hands,
Writ to your Grace from the Duke of Burgundy.

66

20. **but in all I was:** I was in all but.

23. **a trusty squire:** i.e., an untrustworthy follower. **Squire** was sometimes used contemptuously.

26. **surprised:** overcome.

30. **fact:** misdeed.

37. **distress:** difficulty.

38. **most extremes:** utmost straits.

40. **usurp:** assume falsely, without right.

Tal. Shame to the Duke of Burgundy and thee!
I vowed, base knight, when I did meet thee next,
To tear the Garter from thy craven's leg,   15
                              [*Plucking it off.*]
Which I have done, because unworthily
Thou wast installed in that high degree.
Pardon me, princely Henry, and the rest:
This dastard, at the Battle of Patay,
When but in all I was six thousand strong   20
And that the French were almost ten to one,
Before we met or that a stroke was given,
Like to a trusty squire did run away:
In which assault we lost twelve hundred men.
Myself and divers gentlemen beside   25
Were there surprised and taken prisoners.
Then judge, great lords, if I have done amiss;
Or whether that such cowards ought to wear
This ornament of knighthood, yea or no.
    Glou. To say the truth, this fact was infamous   30
And ill beseeming any common man,
Much more a knight, a captain, and a leader.
    Tal. When first this order was ordained, my lords,
Knights of the Garter were of noble birth,
Valiant and virtuous, full of haughty courage,   35
Such as were grown to credit by the wars;
Not fearing death, nor shrinking for distress,
But always resolute in most extremes.
He then that is not furnished in this sort
Doth but usurp the sacred name of knight,   40
Profaning this most honorable order,
And should, if I were worthy to be judge,

43. **hedge-born:** implying beggarly birth.
46. **doom:** judgment.
47. **Be packing:** be off with you.
50. **uncle:** the King's uncle, Bedford, was married to Burgundy's sister.
52. **style:** form of address.
56. **Pretend:** indicate.
72. **abuse:** deceit.

Be quite degraded, like a hedge-born swain
That doth presume to boast of gentle blood.

  King. Stain to thy countrymen, thou hearst thy   45
    doom!

Be packing, therefore, thou that wast a knight.
Henceforth we banish thee, on pain of death.

                         [*Exit Fastolfe.*]

And now, my Lord Protector, view the letter
Sent from our uncle Duke of Burgundy.   50

  Glou. What means His Grace, that he hath changed
    his style?

No more but, plain and bluntly, "To the King!"
Hath he forgot he is his sovereign?
Or doth this churlish superscription   55
Pretend some alteration in good will?
What's here? [*Reads*] "I have, upon especial cause,
Moved with compassion of my country's wrack,
Together with the pitiful complaints
Of such as your oppression feeds upon,   60
Forsaken your pernicious faction
And joined with Charles, the rightful King of France."
O monstrous treachery! can this be so,
That in alliance, amity, and oaths
There should be found such false dissembling guile? 65

  King. What! doth my uncle Burgundy revolt?
  Glou. He doth, my lord, and is become your foe.
  King. Is that the worst this letter doth contain?
  Glou. It is the worst, and all, my lord, he writes.
  King. Why, then, Lord Talbot there shall talk with 70
    him,

And give him chastisement for this abuse.

74-5. **prevented:** forestalled; anticipated.
78. **straight:** immediately.
81. **still:** ever.
82. **confusion:** destruction.
99. **sanguine:** bloody.

How say you, my lord? Are you not content?

   Tal. Content, my Liege! Yes, but that I am prevented,   75

I should have begged I might have been employed.

   King. Then gather strength and march unto him
straight.

Let him perceive how ill we brook his treason

And what offense it is to flout his friends.   80

   Tal. I go, my lord, in heart desiring still

You may behold confusion of your foes.   *[Exit.]*

          Enter Vernon and Basset.

   Ver. Grant me the combat, gracious sovereign.

   Bass. And me, my lord, grant me the combat too.

   York. This is my servant: hear him, noble prince.   85

   Som. And this is mine: sweet Henry, favor him.

   King. Be patient, lords; and give them leave to
speak.

Say, gentlemen, what makes you thus exclaim?

And wherefore crave you combat? or with whom?   90

   Ver. With him, my lord, for he hath done me wrong.

   Bass. And I with him, for he hath done me wrong.

   King. What is that wrong whereof you both com-
plain?

First let me know, and then I'll answer you.   95

   Bass. Crossing the sea from England into France,

This fellow here, with envious carping tongue,

Upbraided me about the rose I wear;

Saying the sanguine color of the leaves

Did represent my master's blushing cheeks   100

101. **repugn:** oppose; deny.

109. **forged quaint conceit:** ingenious false contrivance.

110. **set a gloss upon:** gloss over; conceal.

112. **badge:** the white rose emblem.

114. **Bewrayed:** betrayed.

116. **grudge:** hostility.

121. **emulations:** rivalries.

122. **cousins:** applied generally to close kin other than brothers and sisters.

129. **where it began at first:** i.e., between himself and Basset.

When stubbornly he did repugn the truth
About a certain question in the law
Argued betwixt the Duke of York and him,
With other vile and ignominious terms.
In confutation of which rude reproach,   105
And in defense of my lord's worthiness,
I crave the benefit of law of arms.

   Ver. And that is my petition, noble lord.
For though he seem with forged quaint conceit
To set a gloss upon his bold intent,   110
Yet know, my lord, I was provoked by him;
And he first took exceptions at this badge,
Pronouncing that the paleness of this flower
Bewrayed the faintness of my master's heart.

   York. Will not this malice, Somerset, be left?   115

   Som. Your private grudge, my lord of York, will out,
Though ne'er so cunningly you smother it.

   King. Good Lord, what madness rules in brainsick
    men,
When for so slight and frivolous a cause   120
Such factious emulations shall arise!
Good cousins both, of York and Somerset,
Quiet yourselves, I pray, and be at peace.

   York. Let this dissension first be tried by fight,
And then your Highness shall command a peace.   125

   Som. The quarrel toucheth none but us alone;
Betwixt ourselves let us decide it then.

   York. There is my pledge: accept it, Somerset.

   Ver. Nay, let it rest where it began at first.

   Bass. Confirm it so, mine honorable lord.   130

   Glou. Confirm it so! Confounded be your strife!

134. **immodest:** intemperate.
137. **objections:** contentions.
150. **grudging stomachs:** hostility.
153. **certified:** informed.
154. **toy:** trifle.

And perish ye, with your audacious prate!
Presumptuous vassals, are you not ashamed
With this immodest clamorous outrage
To trouble and disturb the King and us?   135
And you, my lords, methinks you do not well
To bear with their perverse objections;
Much less to take occasion from their mouths
To raise a mutiny betwixt yourselves.
Let me persuade you take a better course.   140

   Exe. It grieves His Highness: good my lords, be
     friends.

   King. Come hither, you that would be combatants.
Henceforth I charge you, as you love our favor,
Quite to forget this quarrel and the cause.   145
And you, my lords, remember where we are:
In France, amongst a fickle wavering nation.
If they perceive dissension in our looks
And that within ourselves we disagree,
How will their grudging stomachs be provoked   150
To willful disobedience and rebell!
Beside, what infamy will there arise
When foreign princes shall be certified
That for a toy, a thing of no regard,
King Henry's peers and chief nobility   155
Destroyed themselves and lost the realm of France!
Oh, think upon the conquest of my father,
My tender years, and let us not forgo
That for a trifle that was bought with blood!
Let me be umpire in this doubtful strife.   160
I see no reason, if I wear this rose,

                      [Putting on a red rose.]

164. **kinsmen:** the King was the great-grandson of John of Gaunt, Somerset the grandson. York was the grandson of Edmund Langley, Gaunt's brother.

176. **digest:** disperse and dispose of.

189. **wist:** knew.

That anyone should therefore be suspicious
I more incline to Somerset than York.
Both are my kinsmen, and I love them both.
As well they may upbraid me with my crown,   165
Because, forsooth, the King of Scots is crowned.
But your discretions better can persuade
Than I am able to instruct or teach:
And therefore, as we hither came in peace,
So let us still continue peace and love.   170
Cousin of York, we institute your Grace
To be our Regent in these parts of France.
And, good my lord of Somerset, unite
Your troops of horsemen with his bands of foot,
And, like true subjects, sons of your progenitors,   175
Go cheerfully together and digest
Your angry choler on your enemies.
Ourself, my Lord Protector, and the rest
After some respite will return to Calais;
From thence to England, where I hope ere long   180
To be presented by your victories
With Charles, Alençon, and that traitorous rout.
[*Flourish.*] *Exeunt. Manent York, Warwick, Exeter,*
and Vernon.

    War. My lord of York, I promise you, the King
Prettily, methought, did play the orator.

    York. And so he did; but yet I like it not,   185
In that he wears the badge of Somerset.

    War. Tush, that was but his fancy, blame him not:
I dare presume, sweet prince, he thought no harm.

    York. And if I wist he did—but let it rest:

201. **But that:** but (also sees) that; **presage:** portend; **event:** outcome.

202. **'Tis much:** it's bad enough.

203. **unkind:** unnatural.

▬▬▬▬▬▬▬▬▬▬▬▬▬▬▬▬▬▬▬▬▬▬▬

IV.[ii.] Talbot presents himself before the walls of Bordeaux, calls upon the general to surrender, and receives a defiant warning that his death is imminent. Realizing that he and his men are surrounded, Talbot exhorts them to sell their lives as dearly as he is resolved to do.

Other affairs must now be managed. 190

Flourish. Exeunt. Manet Exeter.

Exe. Well didst thou, Richard, to suppress thy
voice;
For, had the passions of thy heart burst out,
I fear we should have seen deciphered there
More rancorous spite, more furious raging broils, 195
Than yet can be imagined or supposed.
But howsoe'er, no simple man that sees
This jarring discord of nobility,
This shouldering of each other in the court,
This factious bandying of their favorites, 200
But that it doth presage some ill event.
'Tis much when scepters are in children's hands,
But more when envy breeds unkind division:
There comes the ruin, there begins confusion.

Exit.

[Scene II.] Before Bordeaux.

Enter Talbot, with Trumpet and Drum.

Tal. Go to the gates of Bordeaux, trumpeter;
Summon their general unto the wall.

[Trumpet sounds.]

Enter General [and others,] aloft.

English John Talbot, captains, calls you forth,
Servant in arms to Harry, King of England,

5. **thus he would:** this is what he wants.

8. **bloody power:** forces capable of shedding blood.

11. **quartering:** rending into quarters.

13. **air-braving:** challenging the air.

17. **period:** end.

19. **protest:** attest.

23. **pitched:** arrayed for battle.

25. **redress:** assistance.

26. **front:** face; **apparent spoil:** certain destruction.

29. **rive:** fire.

33. **latest:** last; final.

34. **due:** endow; credit.

And thus he would: open your city gates;   5
Be humble to us; call my sovereign yours
And do him homage as obedient subjects;
And I'll withdraw me and my bloody power:
But, if you frown upon this proffered peace,
You tempt the fury of my three attendants,   10
Lean famine, quartering steel, and climbing fire,
Who in a moment even with the earth
Shall lay your stately and air-braving towers,
If you forsake the offer of their love.

   Gen. Thou ominous and fearful owl of death,   15
Our nation's terror and their bloody scourge,
The period of thy tyranny approacheth.
On us thou canst not enter but by death;
For, I protest, we are well fortified
And strong enough to issue out and fight.   20
If thou retire, the Dauphin, well appointed,
Stands with the snares of war to tangle thee.
On either hand thee there are squadrons pitched,
To wall thee from the liberty of flight;
And no way canst thou turn thee for redress   25
But death doth front thee with apparent spoil
And pale destruction meets thee in the face.
Ten thousand French have ta'en the sacrament
To rive their dangerous artillery
Upon no Christian soul but English Talbot.   30
Lo, there thou standst, a breathing valiant man,
Of an invincible unconquered spirit!
This is the latest glory of thy praise
That I, thy enemy, due thee withal;
For, ere the glass that now begins to run   35

36. **process:** course.

40. **heavy:** woeful.

42. **fables:** lies.

45. **parked and bounded in a pale:** surrounded as in an empaled park.

47. **Mazed:** caught in a maze from which we can find no way out.

48. **be . . . in blood:** perform like animals in prime condition.

49. **rascal-like:** like deer of inferior physical characteristics.

51. **heads of steel:** using weapons as a stag would its horns.

53. **Sell every man:** let every man sell.

Finish the process of his sandy hour,
These eyes, that see thee now well colored,
Shall see thee withered, bloody, pale, and dead.

Drum afar off.

Hark! Hark! the Dauphin's drum, a warning bell,
Sings heavy music to thy timorous soul;   40
And mine shall ring thy dire departure out.

Exeunt [General, etc.]

Tal. He fables not: I hear the enemy.
Out, some light horsemen, and peruse their wings.
Oh, negligent and heedless discipline!
How are we parked and bounded in a pale,   45
A little herd of England's timorous deer,
Mazed with a yelping kennel of French curs!
If we be English deer, be then in blood;
Not rascal-like, to fall down with a pinch,
But rather, moody-mad and desperate stags,   50
Turn on the bloody hounds with heads of steel
And make the cowards stand aloof at bay.
Sell every man his life as dear as mine,
And they shall find dear deer of us, my friends.
God and St. George, Talbot and England's right,   55
Prosper our colors in this dangerous fight!

[Exeunt.]

IV.[iii.] York rages that Somerset has failed to send requested horsemen to accompany his foot soldiers in attempting Talbot's relief. Sir William Lucy brings news of Talbot's plight and urges York to fly to his rescue, but York claims that he cannot move without the horse that Somerset has failed to provide. Lucy contemplates with dismay the rivalries that are costing England the conquests achieved by Henry V.

━━━━━━━━━━━━━━━━━━━━━━━━━

3. **give it out:** report.
14. **louted:** made a fool of.
17. **miscarry:** fail; die.

[Scene III. Plains in Gascony.]

Enter a Messenger that meets York. Enter York with
Trumpet and many Soldiers.

  York. Are not the speedy scouts returned again
That dogged the mighty army of the Dauphin?
  Mess. They are returned, my lord, and give it out
That he is marched to Bordeaux with his power,
To fight with Talbot. As he marched along,   5
By your espials were discovered
Two mightier troops than that the Dauphin led,
Which joined with him and made their march for
    Bordeaux.
  York. A plague upon that villain Somerset,   10
That thus delays my promised supply
Of horsemen that were levied for this siege!
Renowned Talbot doth expect my aid,
And I am louted by a traitor villain
And cannot help the noble chevalier.   15
God comfort him in this necessity!
If he miscarry, farewell wars in France.

Enter [Sir William Lucy].

  Lucy. Thou princely leader of our English strength,
Never so needful on the earth of France,
Spur to the rescue of the noble Talbot,   20
Who now is girdled with a waist of iron
And hemmed about with grim destruction.

26. **cornets:** cavalry companies.

34. **'long:** because.

36. **since:** ago.

48. **sedition:** partisan strife. The image suggests the myth of Prometheus' punishment for helping man against Zeus's wishes. He was doomed to be chained to a rock, where a vulture eternally devoured his liver.

52. **ever-living man of memory:** man of whom the memory will be ever-living.

The punishment of Prometheus' revolt against Zeus. From Geoffrey Whitney, *A Choice of Emblems* (1586).

To Bordeaux, warlike Duke! to Bordeaux, York!
Else, farewell Talbot, France, and England's honor.

    York. O God, that Somerset, who in proud heart   25
Doth stop my cornets, were in Talbot's place!
So should we save a valiant gentleman
By forfeiting a traitor and a coward.
Mad ire and wrathful fury makes me weep
That thus we die while remiss traitors sleep.   30

    Lucy. Oh, send some succor to the distressed lord!

    York. He dies, we lose; I break my warlike word;
We mourn, France smiles; we lose, they daily get;
All 'long of this vile traitor Somerset.

    Lucy. Then God take mercy on brave Talbot's soul;   35
And on his son, young John, who two hours since
I met in travel toward his warlike father!
This seven years did not Talbot see his son,
And now they meet where both their lives are done.

    York. Alas, what joy shall noble Talbot have   40
To bid his young son welcome to his grave?
Away! vexation almost stops my breath
That sundered friends greet in the hour of death.
Lucy, farewell. No more my fortune can,
But curse the cause I cannot aid the man.   45
Maine, Blois, Poitiers, and Tours are won away,
'Long all of Somerset and his delay.

                     Exit, [with his soldiers].

    Lucy. Thus, while the vulture of sedition
Feeds in the bosom of such great commanders,
Sleeping neglection doth betray to loss   50
The conquest of our scarce-cold conqueror,
That ever-living man of memory,

IV.[iv.] Somerset tells one of Talbot's captains that it is too late for him to send the horse needed by Talbot; he accuses York of urging a rash exploit upon Talbot in the hope that his death would remove a rival to York for the glory to be gained in France. Sir William Lucy also appeals to Somerset to aid Talbot. Somerset lays all the blame on York but finally agrees to send the horsemen.

⁙⁙⁙⁙⁙⁙⁙⁙⁙⁙⁙⁙⁙⁙⁙⁙⁙⁙⁙⁙

4-5. Might with a sally of the very town/ Be buckled with: might be coped with by the unassisted forces in the town itself.

9. bear the name: carry off all the honors.

14. bought and sold: betrayed.

Henry the Fifth. Whiles they each other cross,
Lives, honors, lands, and all hurry to loss.

                                        Exit.

[Scene IV. Other plains in Gascony.]

*Enter Somerset, with his army, [a Captain of Talbot's
with him].*

  Som. It is too late; I cannot send them now.
This expedition was by York and Talbot
Too rashly plotted. All our general force
Might with a sally of the very town
Be buckled with. The overdaring Talbot   5
Hath sullied all his gloss of former honor
By this unheedful, desperate, wild adventure.
York set him on to fight and die in shame,
That, Talbot dead, great York might bear the name.
  Capt. Here is Sir William Lucy, who with me   10
Set from our o'ermatched forces forth for aid.

[*Enter Sir William Lucy.*]

  Som. How now, Sir William! Whither were you
    sent?
  Lucy. Whither, my lord? From bought and sold
    Lord Talbot;   15
Who, ringed about with bold adversity,
Cries out for noble York and Somerset
To beat assailing death from his weak legions;

21. **in advantage ling'ring:** holding out in expectation of help.
26. **While:** until.
39. **take foul scorn:** disdain.

And whiles the honorable captain there
Drops bloody sweat from his war-wearied limbs   20
And, in advantage ling'ring, looks for rescue,
You, his false hopes, the trust of England's honor,
Keep off aloof with worthless emulation.
Let not your private discord keep away
The levied succors that should lend him aid,   25
While he, renowned noble gentleman,
Yield up his life unto a world of odds.
Orléans the Bastard, Charles, Burgundy,
Alençon, Reignier, compass him about,
And Talbot perisheth by your default.   30
    Som. York set him on: York should have sent him
        aid.
    Lucy. And York as fast upon your Grace exclaims;
Swearing that you withhold his levied host,
Collected for this expedition.   35
    Som. York lies: he might have sent and had the
        horse,
I owe him little duty, and less love,
And take foul scorn to fawn on him by sending.
    Lucy. The fraud of England, not the force of   40
        France,
Hath now entrapped the noble-minded Talbot.
Never to England shall he bear his life,
But dies, betrayed to fortune by your strife.
    Som. Come, go: I will dispatch the horsemen   45
        straight.
Within six hours they will be at his aid.
    Lucy. Too late comes rescue. He is ta'en or slain;
For fly he could not, if he would have fled;

IV.[v.] Young John Talbot, who has joined his father in his desperate stand, refuses his father's counsel to flee and firmly resolves to fight to the death.

|||||||||||||||||||||||||||||||||||||||||

8. **unavoided:** unavoidable.

And fly would Talbot never, though he might.   50
  Som. If he be dead, brave Talbot, then adieu!
  Lucy. His fame lives in the world, his shame in you.
                                    Exeunt.

[Scene V. The English camp near Bordeaux.]

Enter Talbot and [John] his son.

  Tal. O young John Talbot! I did send for thee
To tutor thee in stratagems of war,
That Talbot's name might be in thee revived
When sapless age and weak unable limbs
Should bring thy father to his drooping chair.   5
But, O malignant and ill-boding stars!
Now thou art come unto a feast of death,
A terrible and unavoided danger.
Therefore, dear boy, mount on my swiftest horse,
And I'll direct thee how thou shalt escape   10
By sudden flight. Come, dally not, be gone.
  John. Is my name Talbot? and am I your son?
And shall I fly? Oh, if you love my mother,
Dishonor not her honorable name,
To make a bastard and a slave of me!   15
The world will say he is not Talbot's blood
That basely fled when noble Talbot stood.
  Tal. Fly, to revenge my death, if I be slain.
  John. He that flies so will ne'er return again.
  Tal. If we both stay, we both are sure to die.   20
  John. Then let me stay, and, father, do you fly.

22. **Your loss is great:** i.e., you would be a great loss; **your regard:** concern for yourself.

28. **vantage:** advantage; hope of gaining a better fighting position.

32. **mortality:** death.

36. **Upon my blessing:** as you hope to have my blessing.

43. **charge:** order; i.e., the fact that his father ordered his flight.

48. **age:** years of life.

Your loss is great, so your regard should be;
My worth unknown, no loss is known in me.
Upon my death the French can little boast;
In yours they will, in you all hopes are lost.   25
Flight cannot stain the honor you have won;
But mine it will, that no exploit have done.
You fled for vantage, everyone will swear;
But if I bow, they'll say it was for fear.
There is no hope that ever I will stay,   30
If the first hour I shrink and run away.
Here on my knee I beg mortality,
Rather than life preserved with infamy.

   Tal. Shall all thy mother's hopes lie in one tomb?
   John. Ay, rather than I'll shame my mother's womb.   35
   Tal. Upon my blessing, I command thee go.
   John. To fight I will, but not to fly the foe.
   Tal. Part of thy father may be saved in thee.
   John. No part of him but will be shame in me.
   Tal. Thou never hadst renown, nor canst not lose it.   40
   John. Yes, your renowned name. Shall flight abuse it?
   Tal. Thy father's charge shall clear thee from that stain.
   John. You cannot witness for me, being slain.   45
If death be so apparent, then both fly.
   Tal. And leave my followers here to fight and die?
My age was never tainted with such shame.
   John. And shall my youth be guilty of such blame?
No more can I be severed from your side   50
Than can yourself yourself in twain divide.
Stay, go, do what you will, the like do I;

IV.[**vi.**] Talbot glories in his son's exploits but tries again to persuade him to leave the scene of battle. His son remains determined to die with his father.

▓▓▓▓▓▓▓▓▓▓▓▓▓▓▓▓▓▓▓▓▓▓▓

3. **France his:** France's.
9. **determined:** predetermined.

Hand-to-hand combat. From Olaus Magnus, *Historia de gentibus septentrionalibus* (1555).

For live I will not, if my father die.

   Tal. Then here I take my leave of thee, fair son,
Born to eclipse thy life this afternoon.   55
Come, side by side together live and die;
And soul with soul from France to Heaven fly.

                            Exeunt.

[Scene VI. A field of battle.]

*Alarum: excursions, wherein Talbot's Son is hemmed
about, and Talbot rescues him.*

   Tal. St. George and victory! Fight, soldiers, fight!
The Regent hath with Talbot broke his word,
And left us to the rage of France his sword.
Where is John Talbot? Pause and take thy breath;
I gave thee life and rescued thee from death.   5

   John. Oh, twice my father, twice am I thy son!
The life thou gavest me first was lost and done,
Till with thy warlike sword, despite of fate,
To my determined time thou gavest new date.

   Tal. When from the Dauphin's crest thy sword   10
     struck fire,
It warmed thy father's heart with proud desire
Of bold-faced victory. Then leaden age,
Quickened with youthful spleen and warlike rage,
Beat down Alençon, Orléans, Burgundy,   15
And from the pride of Gallia rescued thee.
The ireful Bastard Orléans, that drew blood
From thee, my boy, and had the maidenhood
Of thy first fight, I soon encountered,

30. **sealed:** confirmed (by his taste of warfare).

33. **wot:** know.

36. **mickle:** much.

40. **My death's revenge:** the chance that my death may be revenged.

50. **like:** liken.

Icarus falls from the sky. From Andrea Alciati, *Emblemata* (1608). (See lines 56–7, below, and IV. [vii.] 16)

And interchanging blows I quickly shed   20
Some of his bastard blood and in disgrace
Bespoke him thus: "Contaminated, base,
And misbegotten blood I spill of thine,
Mean and right poor, for that pure blood of mine
Which thou didst force from Talbot, my brave boy."   25
Here, purposing the Bastard to destroy,
Came in strong rescue. Speak, thy father's care,
Art thou not weary, John? How dost thou fare?
Wilt thou yet leave the battle, boy, and fly,
Now thou art sealed the son of chivalry?   30
Fly, to revenge my death when I am dead;
The help of one stands me in little stead.
Oh, too much folly is it, well I wot,
To hazard all our lives in one small boat!
If I today die not with Frenchmen's rage,   35
Tomorrow I shall die with mickle age.
By me they nothing gain and if I stay,
'Tis but the short'ning of my life one day.
In thee thy mother dies, our household's name,
My death's revenge, thy youth, and England's fame. 40
All these and more we hazard by thy stay;
All these are saved if thou wilt fly away.
   John. The sword of Orléans hath not made me
      smart;
These words of yours draw lifeblood from my heart. 45
On that advantage, bought with such a shame,
To save a paltry life and slay bright fame,
Before young Talbot from old Talbot fly,
The coward horse that bears me fall and die!
And like me to the peasant boys of France,   50

54. **it is no boot:** it's no use.

56. **sire of Crete:** Daedalus, designer of the Cretan labyrinth, whose son Icarus joined him in his daring escape from Crete by means of wings fastened on with wax. Icarus flew too near the sun and was drowned when the wax melted off his wings and he fell into the sea.

⸻

IV.[vii.] Talbot, mortally wounded, is brought the body of his dead son. His pride in the boy's brave deeds makes death seem a triumph. The Dauphin, accompanied by La Pucelle, Burgundy, and others, comes upon the bodies. Orléans suggests that the bodies be hacked to pieces, but the Dauphin rules that they are due greater respect. Sir William Lucy, coming to inquire about English losses, is shown the dead Talbots and is allowed to bear them off. The French set out for Paris, certain that nothing will stop them now that Talbot is dead.

⸻

3. **Triumphant Death:** Death is triumphant in having conquered Talbot; but Talbot is triumphant in having died bravely in the company of his equally brave son; and their deaths are not accompanied with the disgrace of being captives; **smeared with:** (that would have been) disgraced by.

9. **guardant:** defender.

10. **Tend'ring my ruin:** tenderly caring for me in my ruin.

To be shame's scorn and subject of mischance!
Surely, by all the glory you have won,
And if I fly, I am not Talbot's son.
Then talk no more of flight, it is no boot;
If son to Talbot, die at Talbot's foot.   55

   Tal. Then follow thou thy desp'rate sire of Crete,
Thou Icarus; thy life to me is sweet.
If thou wilt fight, fight by thy father's side;
And, commendable proved, let's die in pride.

                                    Exeunt.

[Scene VII. Another part of the field.]

Alarum: excursions. Enter old Talbot led [by a Serv-
ant].

   Tal. Where is my other life? Mine own is gone.
Oh, where's young Talbot? Where is valiant John?
Triumphant Death, smeared with captivity,
Young Talbot's valor makes me smile at thee.
When he perceived me shrink and on my knee,   5
His bloody sword he brandished over me,
And, like a hungry lion, did commence
Rough deeds of rage and stern impatience;
But when my angry guardant stood alone,
Tend'ring my ruin and assailed of none,   10
Dizzy-eyed fury and great rage of heart
Suddenly made him from my side to start
Into the clust'ring battle of the French;
And in that sea of blood my boy did drench

15. **overmounting:** suggested by Icarus' daring in flying too high.

16. **pride:** prime; flower (of youth).

17. **lo:** behold.

18. **antic:** grinning.

20. **insulting:** exulting.

21. **bonds of perpetuity:** eternal bonds.

22. **lither:** resistless.

23. **In thy despite:** in spite of thee.

24. **hard-favored:** ugly.

26. **Brave:** defy.

28. **as who should say:** like one who would say.

31. **harms:** injuries.

32. **have what I would have:** am content.

36. **wood:** mad.

37. **flesh:** initiate; give a first taste of blood to; **puny:** inexperienced.

His overmounting spirit and there died,   15
My Icarus, my blossom, in his pride.

Enter [Soldiers,] with [the body of young] Talbot.

  Ser. O my dear lord, lo, where your son is borne!
  Tal. Thou antic Death, which laughst us here to
    scorn,
Anon, from thy insulting tyranny,   20
Coupled in bonds of perpetuity,
Two Talbots, winged through the lither sky,
In thy despite shall 'scape mortality.
O thou, whose wounds become hard-favored Death,
Speak to thy father ere thou yield thy breath!   25
Brave Death by speaking, whether he will or no:
Imagine him a Frenchman and thy foe.
Poor boy! he smiles, methinks, as who should say,
Had Death been French, then Death had died today.
Come, come and lay him in his father's arms;   30
My spirit can no longer bear these harms.
Soldiers, adieu! I have what I would have,
Now my old arms are young John Talbot's grave.
                                          Dies.

*Enter Charles, Alençon, Burgundy, Bastard, La Pu-
    celle, [and forces].*

  Char. Had York and Somerset brought rescue in,
We should have found a bloody day of this.   35
  Bas. How the young whelp of Talbot's, raging wood,
Did flesh his puny sword in Frenchmen's blood!

42. **giglet:** wanton.

54. **submissive message:** message of submission.

55-6. **mere French word:** i.e., word known only to the French.

62. **Alcides:** a Greek name for Hercules as grandson of Alcaeus; a champion.

Puc. Once I encountered him, and thus I said:
"Thou maiden youth, be vanquished by a maid."
But, with a proud majestical high scorn,   40
He answered thus: "Young Talbot was not born
To be the pillage of a giglet wench."
So, rushing in the bowels of the French,
He left me proudly, as unworthy fight.

Bur. Doubtless he would have made a noble knight. 45
See, where he lies enhearsed in the arms
Of the most bloody nurser of his harms!

Bas. Hew them to pieces, hack their bones asunder,
Whose life was England's glory, Gallia's wonder.

Char. Oh, no, forbear! For that which we have fled 50
During the life, let us not wrong it dead.

*Enter [Sir William] Lucy, [attended; Herald of the
                French preceding].*

Lucy. Herald, conduct me to the Dauphin's tent,
To know who hath obtained the glory of the day.

Char. On what submissive message art thou sent?

Lucy. Submission, Dauphin! 'Tis a mere French 55
    word:
We English warriors wot not what it means.
I come to know what prisoners thou hast ta'en
And to survey the bodies of the dead.

Char. For prisoners askst thou? Hell our prison is. 60
But tell me whom thou seekst.

Lucy. But where's the great Alcides of the field,
Valiant Lord Talbot, Earl of Shrewsbury,
Created, for his rare success in arms,

75. **silly stately style:** a string of titles so pompous as to be absurd.

81. **Nemesis:** destroyer; literally, a Greek goddess who personified retributive justice.

85. **were:** would be.

87. **amaze:** confound with fear.

90. **upstart:** impudent fellow.

Nemesis, holding the bridle and yoke, symbols of her control of human destiny. From Geoffrey Whitney, *A Choice of Emblems* (1586).

Great Earl of Washford, Waterford, and Valence;   65
Lord Talbot of Goodrig and Urchinfield,
Lord Strange of Blackmere, Lord Verdun of Alton,
Lord Cromwell of Wingfield, Lord Furnivall of Shef-
   field,
The thrice-victorious Lord of Falconbridge;   70
Knight of the noble order of St. George,
Worthy St. Michael, and the Golden Fleece;
Great Marshal to Henry the Sixth
Of all his wars within the realm of France?

   Puc. Here is a silly stately style indeed!   75
The Turk, that two-and-fifty kingdoms hath,
Writes not so tedious a style as this.
Him that thou magnifiest with all these titles
Stinking and flyblown lies here at our feet.

   Lucy. Is Talbot slain, the Frenchmen's only scourge,   80
Your kingdom's terror and black Nemesis?
Oh, were mine eyeballs into bullets turned,
That I in rage might shoot them at your faces!
Oh, that I could but call these dead to life!
It were enough to fright the realm of France.   85
Were but his picture left amongst you here,
It would amaze the proudest of you all.
Give me their bodies, that I may bear them hence
And give them burial as beseems their worth.

   Puc. I think this upstart is old Talbot's ghost,   90
He speaks with such a proud commanding spirit.
For God's sake, let him have 'em: to keep them here,
They would but stink and putrefy the air.

   Char. Go, take their bodies hence.

97. **phoenix:** a legendary bird, reborn from the ashes of its own funeral pyre.

Lucy. I'll bear them hence; but from their ashes   95
    shall be reared
A phoenix that shall make all France afeard.
    Char. So we be rid of them, do with 'em what thou
        wilt.
And now to Paris, in this conquering vein;   100
All will be ours, now bloody Talbot's slain.

                                        Exeunt.

THE FIRST PART
OF
HENRY THE SIXTH

ACT V

[**V.i.**] King Henry agrees to consider terms of peace with France and to marry the daughter of the Earl of Armagnac, with whom a large dowry is offered. Exeter, noting Winchester's garb as a cardinal, expresses a fear that the prelate will be more avid for power. Winchester himself voices his determination to bow to no one.

〰〰〰〰〰〰〰〰〰〰〰

7. **affect:** like; **motion:** suggestion.
13. **immanity:** wicked cruelty.
17. **near knit:** closely related.

[ACT V]

Scene [I. London. The palace.]

Sennet. Enter King, Gloucester, and Exeter.

King. Have you perused the letters from the Pope,
The Emperor, and the Earl of Armagnac?
Glou. I have, my lord, and their intent is this:
They humbly sue unto your Excellence
To have a godly peace concluded of   5
Between the realms of England and of France.
King. How doth your Grace affect their motion?
Glou. Well, my good lord; and as the only means
To stop effusion of our Christian blood
And stablish quietness on every side.   10
King. Ay, marry, uncle; for I always thought
It was both impious and unnatural
That such immanity and bloody strife
Should reign among professors of one faith.
Glou. Beside, my lord, the sooner to effect   15
And surer bind this knot of amity,
The Earl of Armagnac, near knit to Charles,
A man of great authority in France,
Proffers his only daughter to your Grace

35. **several:** separate.

In marriage, with a large and sumptuous dowry.   20
 King. Marriage, uncle! alas, my years are young!
And fitter is my study and my books
Than wanton dalliance with a paramour.
Yet call the ambassadors; and, as you please,
So let them have their answers every one.   25
I shall be well content with any choice
Tends to God's glory and my country's weal.

*Enter Winchester [in Cardinal's habit, a Legate], and
   two Ambassadors.*

 Exe. [*Aside*] What! is my lord of Winchester in-
  stalled,
And called unto a cardinal's degree?   30
Then I perceive that will be verified
Henry the Fifth did sometime prophesy:
"If once he come to be a cardinal,
He'll make his cap co-equal with the crown."
 King. My lords ambassadors, your several suits   35
Have been considered and debated on.
Your purpose is both good and reasonable;
And therefore are we certainly resolved
To draw conditions of a friendly peace;
Which by my lord of Winchester we mean   40
Shall be transported presently to France.
 Glou. And for the proffer of my lord your master,
I have informed His Highness so at large,
As, liking of the lady's virtuous gifts,
Her beauty, and the value of her dower,   45
He doth intend she shall be England's queen.

47. **In argument and proof:** as evidence in proof.

58. **trow:** declare.

64. **mutiny:** rebellion.

━━━━━━━━━━━━━━━━━━━━━━━━━━━━━━━

[**V.ii.**] The Dauphin and his party, marching to Paris, receive a message that the English forces have joined together and threaten immediate battle.

King. In argument and proof of which contract,
Bear her this jewel, pledge of my affection.
And so, my Lord Protector, see them guarded
And safely brought to Dover, where, enshipped,   50
Commit them to the fortune of the sea.

                    Exeunt [all but Winchester and Legate].

Win. Stay, my lord legate. You shall first receive
The sum of money which I promised
Should be delivered to His Holiness
For clothing me in these grave ornaments.   55

Leg. I will attend upon your Lordship's leisure.

Win. [*Aside*] Now Winchester will not submit, I
    trow,
Or be inferior to the proudest peer.
Humphrey of Gloucester, thou shalt well perceive   60
That, neither in birth or for authority,
The Bishop will be overborne by thee.
I'll either make thee stoop and bend thy knee,
Or sack this country with a mutiny.

                                        Exeunt.

Scene [II. France. Plains in Anjou.]

*Enter Charles, Burgundy, Alençon, Bastard, Reignier,
        La Pucelle, [and forces].*

Char. These news, my lords, may cheer our droop-
    ing spirits:
'Tis said the stout Parisians do revolt
And turn again unto the warlike French.

20. **passions:** emotions.
21. **Command:** if thou command.

━━━━━━━━━━━━━━━━━━━━━━━━━━━━━━━

[V.]iii. La Pucelle finds her power deserting her and in vain implores the help of her evil spirits, who shake their heads and will not do her bidding. She foresees that France will again fall into England's power. In confirmation of her words, the French are routed and she is captured by the Duke of York. The Earl of Suffolk takes prisoner Margaret, daughter of Reignier, King of Naples and Duke of Anjou. Suffolk, entranced with her beauty and charm, conceives a sudden plan to woo her, ostensibly for King Henry, but actually for himself. He tells her father that he has persuaded the King to marry Margaret, and Reignier gives his consent on condition that Maine and Anjou be restored to him. Suffolk inveigles a kiss from Margaret as a token for the King. He plans to sing her praises so that the King will be unable to resist the prospect of such a marriage.

━━━━━━━━━━━━━━━━━━━━━━━━━━━━━━━

2. **periapts:** amulets.

Alen. Then march to Paris, royal Charles of France,   5
And keep not back your powers in dalliance.

Puc. Peace be amongst them, if they turn to us;
Else, ruin combat with their palaces!

Enter Scout.

Scout. Success unto our valiant general,
And happiness to his accomplices!   10

Char. What tidings send our scouts? I prithee,
      speak.

Scout. The English army, that divided was
Into two parties, is now conjoined in one
And means to give you battle presently.   15

Char. Somewhat too sudden, sirs, the warning is;
But we will presently provide for them.

Bur. I trust the ghost of Talbot is not there:
Now he is gone, my lord, you need not fear.

Puc. Of all base passions, fear is most accursed.   20
Command the conquest, Charles, it shall be thine,
Let Henry fret and all the world repine.

Char. Then on, my lords; and France be fortunate!
                              Exeunt.

Scene III. [Before Angers.]

Alarum. Excursions. Enter La Pucelle.

Puc. The Regent conquers, and the Frenchmen fly.
Now help, ye charming spells and periapts;

3. **admonish:** advise.

4. **accidents:** happenings.

5. **substitutes:** subordinates.

6. **the lordly monarch of the North:** the controller of evil spirits. The North was believed to be their particular abode.

10. **culled:** gathered.

14. **Where:** whereas.

16. **earnest:** token payment.

18. **redress:** aid.

23. **foil:** overthrow; defeat.

25. **vail:** bow.

And ye choice spirits that admonish me
And give me signs of future accidents.   *Thunder.*
You speedy helpers that are substitutes   5
Under the lordly monarch of the North,
Appear and aid me in this enterprise.

Enter Fiends.

This speedy and quick appearance argues proof
Of your accustomed diligence to me.
Now, ye familiar spirits, that are culled   10
Out of the powerful regions under earth,
Help me this once, that France may get the field.
                 They walk, and speak not.
Oh, hold me not with silence overlong!
Where I was wont to feed you with my blood,
I'll lop a member off and give it you   15
In earnest of a further benefit,
So you do condescend to help me now.
                 They hang their heads.
No hope to have redress? My body shall
Pay recompense, if you will grant my suit.
                 They shake their heads.
Cannot my body nor blood sacrifice   20
Entreat you to your wonted furtherance?
Then take my soul, my body, soul and all,
Before that England give the French the foil.
                 They depart.
See, they forsake me! Now the time is come
That France must vail her lofty-plumed crest   25
And let her head fall into England's lap.

28. **buckle:** struggle; grapple.

34. **bend:** knit.

35. **with:** like; **Circe:** the enchantress encountered by Odysseus, who changed men to animals by means of a potion.

37. **proper:** handsome.

42. **Fell:** deadly; **banning:** cursing.

Circe and men transformed to beasts. From Geoffrey Whitney, *A Choice of Emblems* (1586).

My ancient incantations are too weak
And hell too strong for me to buckle with.
Now, France, thy glory droopeth to the dust.

*Excursions. [Enter] Burgundy and York fight[ing]
hand to hand: [La Pucelle is taken. The] French fly.*

York. Damsel of France, I think I have you fast.   30
Unchain your spirits now with spelling charms,
And try if they can gain your liberty.
A goodly prize, fit for the Devil's grace!
See, how the ugly witch doth bend her brows,
As if with Circe she would change my shape!   35
    Puc. Changed to a worser shape thou canst not be.
    York. Oh, Charles the Dauphin is a proper man:
No shape but his can please your dainty eye.
    Puc. A plaguing mischief light on Charles and thee!
And may ye both be suddenly surprised   40
By bloody hands, in sleeping on your beds!
    York. Fell banning hag, enchantress, hold thy
        tongue!
    Puc. I prithee, give me leave to curse awhile.
    York. Curse, miscreant, when thou comest to the   45
        stake.   *Exeunt.*

Alarum. Enter Suffolk with Margaret in his hand.

Suf. Be what thou wilt, thou art my prisoner.
                                Gazes on her.
O fairest beauty, do not fear nor fly!
For I will touch thee but with reverent hands:

64. **glassy:** mirrorlike.

69. **disable:** disparage.

73. **Confounds the tongue and makes the senses rough:** destroys the power of speech and disturbs the senses.

I kiss these fingers for eternal peace,   50
And lay them gently on thy tender side.
Who art thou? Say, that I may honor thee.
 Mar. Margaret my name, and daughter to a king,
The King of Naples, whosoe'er thou art.
  Suf. An earl I am, and Suffolk am I called.   55
Be not offended, nature's miracle,
Thou art allotted to be ta'en by me.
So doth the swan her downy cygnets save,
Keeping them prisoner underneath her wings.
Yet, if this servile usage once offend,   60
Go and be free again as Suffolk's friend. *She is going.*
Oh, stay! [*Aside*] I have no power to let her pass:
My hand would free her, but my heart says no.
As plays the sun upon the glassy streams,
Twinkling another counterfeited beam,   65
So seems this gorgeous beauty to mine eyes.
Fain would I woo her, yet I dare not speak.
I'll call for pen and ink and write my mind.
Fie, De la Pole! disable not thyself:
Hast not a tongue? Is she not here?   70
Wilt thou be daunted at a woman's sight?
Ay, beauty's princely majesty is such,
Confounds the tongue and makes the senses rough.
 Mar. Say, Earl of Suffolk—if thy name be so—
What ransom must I pay before I pass?   75
For I perceive I am thy prisoner.
  Suf. [*Aside*] How canst thou tell she will deny thy
   suit,
Before thou make a trial of her love?

86. **Fond:** foolish.

91-2. **cooling card:** i.e., something that thwarts one's hopes; the phrase is proverbial.

101. **fancy:** love.

103. **scruple:** uncertainty.

Mar. Why speakst thou not? What ransom must I   80
    pay?

Suf. [*Aside*] She's beautiful and therefore to be
    wooed;

She is a woman, therefore to be won.

    Mar. Wilt thou accept of ransom?—yea, or no.   85

    Suf. [*Aside*] Fond man, remember that thou hast a
    wife;

Then how can Margaret be thy paramour?

    Mar. [*Aside*] I were best to leave him, for he will
    not hear.   90

    Suf. [*Aside*] There all is marred; there lies a cooling
    card.

    Mar. [*Aside*] He talks at random; sure, the man is
    mad.

    Suf. [*Aside*] And yet a dispensation may be had.   95

    Mar. And yet I would that you would answer me.

    Suf. [*Aside*] I'll win this Lady Margaret. For
    whom?

Why, for my king. Tush, that's a wooden thing!

    Mar. [*Aside*] He talks of wood: it is some carpenter.   100

    Suf. [*Aside*] Yet so my fancy may be satisfied

And peace established between these realms.

But there remains a scruple in that too;

For though her father be the King of Naples,

Duke of Anjou and Maine, yet is he poor,   105

And our nobility will scorn the match.

    Mar. Hear ye, captain, are you not at leisure?

    Suf. [*Aside*] It shall be so, disdain they ne'er so
    much.

Henry is youthful and will quickly yield—   110

112. **enthralled:** captured.

123. **quid for quo:** tit for tat; an even exchange (for his failure to heed her words).

141. **no portion in the choice:** no share in the choosing or in the possession of the thing chosen.

Madam, I have a secret to reveal.

  Mar. [*Aside*] What though I be enthralled? He
    seems a knight,

And will not any way dishonor me.

  Suf. Lady, vouchsafe to listen what I say.   115

  Mar. [*Aside*] Perhaps I shall be rescued by the
    French;

And then I need not crave his courtesy.

  Suf. Sweet madam, give me hearing in a cause—

  Mar. [*Aside*] Tush, women have been captivate ere 120
    now.

  Suf. Lady, wherefore talk you so?

  Mar. I cry you mercy, 'tis but *quid* for *quo.*

  Suf. Say, gentle princess, would you not suppose

Your bondage happy, to be made a queen?   125

  Mar. To be a queen in bondage is more vile

Than is a slave in base servility:

For princes should be free.

  Suf.   And so shall you,

If happy England's royal king be free.   130

  Mar. Why, what concerns his freedom unto me?

  Suf. I'll undertake to make thee Henry's queen,

To put a golden scepter in thy hand

And set a precious crown upon thy head,

If thou wilt condescend to be my—   135

  Mar.   What?

  Suf. His love.

  Mar. I am unworthy to be Henry's wife.

  Suf. No, gentle madam; I unworthy am

To woo so fair a dame to be his wife,   140

And have no portion in the choice myself.

144. **colors:** standards; flags.
161. **face:** pretend.
163. **just:** honest.

How say you, madam, are ye so content?
   Mar. And if my father please, I am content.
   Suf. Then call our captains and our colors forth.
And, madam, at your father's castle walls   145
We'll crave a parley, to confer with him.
                                [*A parley sounded.*]

          Enter Reignier [*on the walls*].

See, Reignier, see, thy daughter prisoner!
   Reign. To whom?
   Suf.   To me.
   Reign.   Suffolk, what remedy?   150
I am a soldier and unapt to weep
Or to exclaim on fortune's fickleness.
   Suf. Yes, there is remedy enough, my lord.
Consent, and for thy honor give consent,
Thy daughter shall be wedded to my king;   155
Whom I with pain have wooed and won thereto;
And this her easy-held imprisonment
Hath gained thy daughter princely liberty.
   Reign. Speaks Suffolk as he thinks?
   Suf.   Fair Margaret knows 160
That Suffolk doth not flatter, face, or feign.
   Reign. Upon thy princely warrant, I descend
To give thee answer of thy just demand.
                        [*Exit from the walls.*]
   Suf. And here I will expect thy coming.

167. **happy:** fortunate; **for:** in having.
179. **again:** in exchange.
189. **becomes:** is appropriate.

Trumpets sound. Enter Reignier [below].

Reign. Welcome, brave Earl, into our territories. 165
Command in Anjou what your Honor pleases.

  Suf. Thanks, Reignier, happy for so sweet a child,
Fit to be made companion with a king.
What answer makes your Grace unto my suit?

  Reign. Since thou dost deign to woo her little worth 170
To be the princely bride of such a lord;
Upon condition I may quietly
Enjoy mine own, the country Maine and Anjou,
Free from oppression or the stroke of war,
My daughter shall be Henry's, if he please. 175

  Suf. That is her ransom: I deliver her,
And those two counties I will undertake
Your Grace shall well and quietly enjoy.

  Reign. And I again, in Henry's royal name,
As deputy unto that gracious king, 180
Give thee her hand, for sign of plighted faith.

  Suf. Reignier of France, I give thee kingly thanks,
Because this is in traffic of a king.
[Aside] And yet, methinks, I could be well content
To be mine own attorney in this case.— 185
I'll over then to England with this news,
And make this marriage to be solemnized.
So farewell, Reignier. Set this diamond safe
In golden palaces, as it becomes.

  Reign. I do embrace thee, as I would embrace 190
The Christian prince, King Henry, were he here.

207. **peevish:** childish.

210. **Minotaurs:** perils like the Minotaur of the Cretan labyrinth that Theseus slew.

212. **surmount:** exceed (those of others).

213. **extinguish:** outshine.

214. **Repeat their semblance often on the seas:** recite them to yourself during the return voyage (so as to know them by heart).

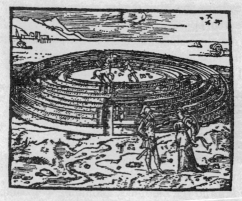

Theseus and Ariadne outside the labyrinth where the Minotaur lurks. From Claude Menestrier, *L'art des emblemes* (1684).

Mar. Farewell, my lord. Good wishes, praise, and
   prayers
Shall Suffolk ever have of Margaret.   *She is going.*
   Suf. Farewell, sweet madam: but hark you, Mar- 195
   garet—
No princely commendations to my king?
   Mar. Such commendations as becomes a maid,
A virgin, and his servant say to him.
   Suf. Words sweetly placed and modestly directed. 200
But, madam, I must trouble you again:
No loving token to His Majesty?
   Mar. Yes, my good lord, a pure unspotted heart,
Never yet taint with love, I send the King.
   Suf. And this withal.   *Kisses her.* 205
   Mar. That for thyself: I will not so presume
To send such peevish tokens to a king.
           [Exeunt Reignier and Margaret.]
   Suf. Oh, wert thou for myself! But, Suffolk, stay.
Thou mayst not wander in that labyrinth:
There Minotaurs and ugly treasons lurk.   210
Solicit Henry with her wondrous praise;
Bethink thee on her virtues that surmount
And natural graces that extinguish art;
Repeat their semblance often on the seas,
That, when thou comest to kneel at Henry's feet,   215
Thou mayst bereave him of his wits with wonder.
                  Exit.

[V.iv.] A shepherd, claiming to be La Pucelle's father, is brought to the English camp where she is a prisoner. She denies being his daughter and claims royal descent and divine inspiration. Cursing her, the shepherd declares that hanging is too good for her and suggests that she should be burnt, a fate already prepared for her. Warwick orders that her ordeal be shortened by plentiful faggots and the addition of pitch. Despairing of mercy, La Pucelle claims to be pregnant and names one after another of the French nobles until her captors sarcastically comment that, with so many lovers, she cannot name the child's father. After she has been led off to the stake, Winchester arrives with the King's commission to arrange a peace with the French. The Dauphin, reluctant to lose the advantage of complete power gained by conquest, is finally persuaded by Alençon and Reignier to accept the terms.

5. **timeless:** untimely.

7. **miser:** miserable one.

10. **and please:** if it please.

17. **obstacle:** obstinate.

18. **collop:** morsel; this refers to the proverb "It is a dear collop that is taken out of the flesh."

21. **suborned:** bribed to lie.

23. **noble:** a coin, valued at 6s.8d. in Shakespeare's time.

[Scene IV. Camp of the Duke of York in Anjou.]

Enter York, Warwick, and [others].

York. Bring forth that sorceress condemned to burn.

Enter La Pucelle, [guarded, and a] Shepherd.

Shep. Ah, Joan, this kills thy father's heart outright!
Have I sought every country far and near,
And, now it is my chance to find thee out,
Must I behold thy timeless, cruel death?   5
Ah, Joan, sweet daughter Joan, I'll die with thee!
    Puc. Decrepit miser; base ignoble wretch!
I am descended of a gentler blood.
Thou art no father nor no friend of mine.
    Shep. Out, out! My lords, and please you, 'tis not so;   10
I did beget her, all the parish knows.
Her mother liveth yet, can testify
She was the first fruit of my bach'lorship.
    War. Graceless! wilt thou deny thy parentage?
    York. This argues what her kind of life hath been,   15
Wicked and vile; and so her death concludes.
    Shep. Fie, Joan, that thou wilt be so obstacle!
God knows thou art a collop of my flesh,
And for thy sake have I shed many a tear.
Deny me not, I prithee, gentle Joan.   20
    Puc. Peasant, avaunt! You have suborned this man,
Of purpose to obscure my noble birth.
    Shep. 'Tis true, I gave a noble to the priest

47. **want:** lack.
49. **compass:** achieve.
53. **effused:** shed.

The morn that I was wedded to her mother.
Kneel down and take my blessing, good my girl.   25
Wilt thou not stoop? Now cursed be the time
Of thy nativity! I would the milk
Thy mother gave thee when thou suck'dst her breast
Had been a little ratsbane for thy sake!
Or else, when thou didst keep my lambs afield,   30
I wish some ravenous wolf had eaten thee!
Dost thou deny thy father, cursed drab?
Oh, burn her, burn her! hanging is too good.   *Exit.*
    York. Take her away; for she hath lived too long,
To fill the world with vicious qualities.   35
    Puc. First, let me tell you whom you have con-
        demned:
Not one begotten of a shepherd swain,
But issued from the progeny of kings,
Virtuous and holy, chosen from above,   40
By inspiration of celestial grace,
To work exceeding miracles on earth.
I never had to do with wicked spirits;
But you, that are polluted with your lusts,
Stained with the guiltless blood of innocents,   45
Corrupt and tainted with a thousand vices,
Because you want the grace that others have,
You judge it straight a thing impossible
To compass wonders but by help of devils.
No, misconceived! Joan of Arc hath been   50
A virgin from her tender infancy,
Chaste and immaculate in very thought;
Whose maiden blood, thus rigorously effused,
Will cry for vengeance at the gates of Heaven.

57. **enow:** enough.

61. **discover:** reveal.

62. **warranteth:** guarantees; **privilege:** immunity. Usually a pregnant woman had her execution stayed until the birth of the child.

66. **forfend:** forbid.

69. **preciseness:** puritanism; chastity.

70. **juggling:** engaging in love play.

72. **go to:** say no more.

73. **father it:** acknowledge himself its father.

76. **notorious Machiavel:** an anachronistic identification of the fifteenth-century Alençon with the contemporary Duke whose courtship of Queen Elizabeth was unpopular in England and to whom Innocent Gentillet dedicated his French translation of Machiavelli's *Il principe*.

78. **give me leave:** pardon me.

84. **liberal:** licentious.

York. Ay, ay. Away with her to execution!   55
War. And hark ye, sirs, because she is a maid,
Spare for no faggots, let there be enow.
Place barrels of pitch upon the fatal stake,
That so her torture may be shortened.
Puc. Will nothing turn your unrelenting hearts?   60
Then, Joan, discover thine infirmity,
That warranteth by law to be thy privilege.
I am with child, ye bloody homicides.
Murder not then the fruit within my womb,
Although ye hale me to a violent death.   65
York. Now Heaven forfend! the holy maid with
    child!
War. The greatest miracle that e'er ye wrought.
Is all your strict preciseness come to this?
York. She and the Dauphin have been juggling.   70
I did imagine what would be her refuge.
War. Well, go to: we'll have no bastards live,
Especially since Charles must father it.
Puc. You are deceived: my child is none of his:
It was Alençon that enjoyed my love.   75
York. Alençon! that notorious Machiavel!
It dies and if it had a thousand lives.
Puc. Oh, give me leave, I have deluded you.
'Twas neither Charles, nor yet the Duke I named,
But Reignier, King of Naples, that prevailed.   80
War. A married man! that's most intolerable.
York. Why, here's a girl! I think she knows not well,
There were so many, whom she may accuse.
War. It's sign she hath been liberal and free.
York. And yet, forsooth, she is a virgin pure.   85

90. **reflex:** reflect.
93. **mischief:** misfortune.
96. **minister:** agent.
100. **remorse:** compassion.
104. **some matter:** details.
105. **effect:** result.

Strumpet, thy words condemn thy brat and thee.
Use no entreaty, for it is in vain.

    Puc. Then lead me hence; with whom I leave my
      curse.
May never glorious sun reflex his beams   90
Upon the country where you make abode;
But darkness and the gloomy shade of death
Environ you, till mischief and despair
Drive you to break your necks or hang yourselves!
                              Exit, [*guarded*].

    York. Break thou in pieces and consume to ashes,   95
Thou foul accursed minister of hell!

Enter Cardinal [*Beaufort, Bishop of Winchester,
attended*].

    Car. Lord Regent, I do greet your Excellence
With letters of commission from the King.
For know, my lords, the states of Christendom,
Moved with remorse of these outrageous broils,   100
Have earnestly implored a general peace
Betwixt our nation and the aspiring French;
And here at hand the Dauphin and his train
Approacheth, to confer about some matter.

    York. Is all our travail turned to this effect?   105
After the slaughter of so many peers,
So many captains, gentlemen, and soldiers
That in this quarrel have been overthrown
And sold their bodies for their country's benefit,
Shall we at last conclude effeminate peace?   110
Have we not lost most part of all the towns,

118. **As:** that.

123. **choler:** anger.

124-25. **poisoned vóice,/ By sight:** i.e., voice, poisoned by sight.

127. **in regard:** considering that.

128. **Of:** out of.

138. **substance and authority:** real authority.

By treason, falsehood, and by treachery,
Our great progenitors had conquered?
O Warwick, Warwick! I foresee with grief
The utter loss of all the realm of France.   115

 War. Be patient, York. If we conclude a peace,
It shall be with such strict and severe covenants
As little shall the Frenchmen gain thereby.

*Enter Charles, Alençon, Bastard, Reignier, [and
    others].*

 Char. Since, lords of England, it is thus agreed
That peaceful truce shall be proclaimed in France, 120
We come to be informed by yourselves
What the conditions of that league must be.

 York. Speak, Winchester, for boiling choler chokes
The hollow passage of my poisoned voice,
By sight of these our baleful enemies.   125

 Car. Charles, and the rest, it is enacted thus:
That, in regard King Henry gives consent,
Of mere compassion and of lenity,
To ease your country of distressful war
And suffer you to breathe in fruitful peace, 130
You shall become true liegemen to his crown.
And, Charles, upon condition thou wilt swear
To pay him tribute and submit thyself,
Thou shalt be placed as viceroy under him
And still enjoy thy regal dignity.   135

 Alen. Must he be then as shadow of himself?
Adorn his temples with a coronet
And yet, in substance and authority,

139. **but privilege of a private man:** no more privilege than an ordinary citizen.

144. **lucre:** gain; **unvanquished:** not recaptured.

148-49. **coveting for more,/ Be cast from possibility of all:** compare the proverb "All covet, all lose."

150. **Insulting:** arrogant.

152. **grows to compromise:** approaches arbitration.

153. **upon comparison:** as a result of comparing your present status with that which we offer.

155. **Of benefit:** as a gift.

156. **of any challenge of desert:** proceeding from any claim of merit.

161. **neglected:** refused.

164. **policy:** shrewdest course.

Retain but privilege of a private man?
This proffer is absurd and reasonless.   140

   Char. 'Tis known already that I am possessed
With more than half the Gallian territories
And therein reverenced for their lawful king.
Shall I, for lucre of the rest unvanquished,
Detract so much from that prerogative   145
As to be called but viceroy of the whole?
No, lord ambassador, I'll rather keep
That which I have, than, coveting for more,
Be cast from possibility of all.

   York. Insulting Charles! hast thou by secret means 150
Used intercession to obtain a league,
And, now the matter grows to compromise,
Standst thou aloof upon comparison?
Either accept the title thou usurpst,
Of benefit proceeding from our King   155
And not of any challenge of desert,
Or we will plague thee with incessant wars.

   Reign. [*Aside to Charles*] My lord, you do not well
     in obstinacy
To cavil in the course of this contract.   160
If once it be neglected, ten to one
We shall not find like opportunity.

   Alen. [*Aside to Charles*] To say the truth, it is your
     policy
To save your subjects from such massacre   165
And ruthless slaughters as are daily seen
By our proceeding in hostility;
And therefore take this compact of a truce,
Although you break it when your pleasure serves.

180. **ensigns:** battle flags.
181. **entertain:** accept.

▪▪

[**V.v.**] Suffolk's description of Margaret of Anjou
stirs the King's fancy to passionate love. Gloucester
objects that the King is contracted to another lady
of equal rank and Exeter adds that Armagnac's daughter also brings a dowry. To this Suffolk replies that
it is beneath the dignity of England's king to marry
for any consideration except pure love. Having en-
snared the King's heart, Suffolk jubilantly prepares
himself to set out for France, as Paris did to Greece.
He hopes that his ultimate success will be better than
that of the Trojan prince: if all goes well, Queen
Margaret will rule the King, and Suffolk will rule
her and the realm.

▪▪▪▪▪▪▪▪▪▪▪▪▪▪▪▪▪▪▪▪▪▪▪▪▪▪▪▪▪▪▪▪

2. **astonished:** stunned.
6. **Provokes:** urges.
7. **breath:** breathing; report.

War. How sayst thou, Charles? Shall our condition   170
    stand?
    Char. It shall;
Only reserved, you claim no interest
In any of our towns of garrison.
    York. Then swear allegiance to His Majesty,   175
As thou art knight, never to disobey
Nor be rebellious to the crown of England,
Thou, nor thy nobles, to the crown of England.
        [Charles and the rest give tokens of fealty.]
So, now dismiss your army when ye please,
Hang up your ensigns, let your drums be still,   180
For here we entertain a solemn peace.
                          Exeunt.

[Scene] V. [London. The royal palace.]

Enter Suffolk, in conference with the King, Glouces-
ter, and Exeter.

    King. Your wondrous rare description, noble Earl,
Of beauteous Margaret hath astonished me.
Her virtues, graced with external gifts,
Do breed love's settled passions in my heart;
And like as rigor of tempestuous gusts   5
Provokes the mightiest hulk against the tide,
So am I driven by breath of her renown,
Either to suffer shipwrack or arrive
Where I may have fruition of her love.
    Suf. Tush, my good lord, this superficial tale   10

11. **her worthy praise:** the praise she merits.
15. **conceit:** imagination; intelligence.
17. **full-replete:** completely furnished.
25. **flatter:** encourage.
31. **triumph:** tournament.
33. **odds:** inferior skill.
39. **glorious:** ostentatious.

Is but a preface of her worthy praise.
The chief perfections of that lovely dame,
Had I sufficient skill to utter them,
Would make a volume of enticing lines,
Able to ravish any dull conceit.   15
And, which is more, she is not so divine,
So full-replete with choice of all delights,
But with as humble lowliness of mind
She is content to be at your command;
Command, I mean, of virtuous chaste intents,   20
To love and honor Henry as her lord.
    King. And otherwise will Henry ne'er presume.
Therefore, my Lord Protector, give consent
That Marg'ret may be England's royal queen.
    Glou. So should I give consent to flatter sin.   25
You know, my lord, your Highness is betrothed
Unto another lady of esteem.
How shall we then dispense with that contract,
And not deface your honor with reproach?
    Suf. As doth a ruler with unlawful oaths,   30
Or one that, at a triumph having vowed
To try his strength, forsaketh yet the lists
By reason of his adversary's odds.
A poor earl's daughter is unequal odds,
And therefore may be broke without offense.   35
    Glou. Why, what, I pray, is Margaret more than
      that?
Her father is no better than an earl,
Although in glorious titles he excel.
    Suf. Yes, my lord, her father is a king,   40
The King of Naples and Jerusalem;

43. **confirm:** make firmer.

47. **liberal:** generous.

52. **perfect:** pure; unalloyed by other considerations.

58. **attorneyship:** proxy. The meaning is that the matter is one to be decided by the King without regard to the advocacy of his counselors.

59. **affects:** prefers.

70. **feature:** comeliness.

71. **Approves:** proves; confirms.

And of such great authority in France
As his alliance will confirm our peace
And keep the Frenchmen in allegiance.

    Glou. And so the Earl of Armagnac may do,   45
Because he is near kinsman unto Charles.

    Exe. Beside, his wealth doth warrant a liberal
      dower,
Where Reignier sooner will receive than give.

    Suf. A dow'r, my lords! Disgrace not so your king,   50
That he should be so abject, base, and poor
To choose for wealth and not for perfect love.
Henry is able to enrich his queen,
And not to seek a queen to make him rich.
So worthless peasants bargain for their wives,   55
As marketmen for oxen, sheep, or horse.
Marriage is a matter of more worth
Than to be dealt in by attorneyship.
Not whom we will, but whom His Grace affects,
Must be companion of his nuptial bed.   60
And therefore, lords, since he affects her most,
It most of all these reasons bindeth us
In our opinions she should be preferred.
For what is wedlock forced but a hell,
An age of discord and continual strife?   65
Whereas the contrary bringeth bliss
And is a pattern of celestial peace.
Whom should we match with Henry, being a king,
But Margaret, that is daughter to a king?
Her peerless feature, joined with her birth,   70
Approves her fit for none but for a king.
Her valiant courage and undaunted spirit,

74. **issue of a king:** i.e., birth of an heir to the throne.

82. **for that:** because.

83. **attaint:** attainted; touched.

89. **post:** speed.

94. **expenses and sufficient charge:** sufficient money to pay expenses.

95. **Among the people gather up a tenth:** i.e., levy a tax on the people's income.

97. **rest:** remain.

99. **censure:** judge; **what you were:** i.e., the youth you once were. Historically, Gloucester's many love affairs were notorious.

101. **will:** a common meaning is "sexual desire."

103. **revolve and ruminate:** mull over.

More than in women commonly is seen,
Will answer our hope in issue of a king:
For Henry, son unto a conqueror,   75
Is likely to beget more conquerors,
If with a lady of so high resolve
As is fair Margaret he be linked in love.
Then yield, my lords; and here conclude with me
That Margaret shall be Queen, and none but she.   80
    King. Whether it be through force of your report,
My noble lord of Suffolk, or for that
My tender youth was never yet attaint
With any passion of inflaming love,
I cannot tell; but this I am assured,   85
I feel such sharp dissension in my breast,
Such fierce alarums both of hope and fear,
As I am sick with working of my thoughts.
Take, therefore, shipping; post, my lord, to France;
Agree to any covenants, and procure   90
That Lady Margaret do vouchsafe to come
To cross the seas to England and be crowned
King Henry's faithful and anointed queen.
For your expenses and sufficient charge,
Among the people gather up a tenth.   95
Be gone, I say: for, till you do return,
I rest perplexed with a thousand cares.
And you, good uncle, banish all offense.
If you do censure me by what you were,
Not what you are, I know it will excuse   100
This sudden execution of my will.
And so, conduct me where, from company,
I may revolve and ruminate my grief.   *Exit.*

106. **Paris:** the Trojan prince who abducted Helen and caused the Trojan war, in which he was killed.

Glou. Ay, grief, I fear me, both at first and last.

                        Exeunt Gloucester [and Exeter].

Suf. Thus Suffolk hath prevailed; and thus he goes,   105
As did the youthful Paris once to Greece,
With hope to find the like event in love
But prosper better than the Trojan did.
Margaret shall now be Queen and rule the King;
But I will rule both her, the King, and realm.   110

                                     Exit.

KEY TO

Famous Passages

Hung be the heavens with black, yield day
   to night!   [*Bedford*—I. i. 1-2]

These news would cause him once more
   yield the ghost.   [*Gloucester*—I. i. 73-4]

Fight till the last gasp.   [*Pucelle*—I. [ii.] 139]

Expect St. Martin's summer, halcyon's days.
                            [*Pucelle*—I. [ii.] 143]

Glory is like a circle in the water,
Which never ceaseth to enlarge itself
Till by broad spreading it disperse to nought.
                      [*Pucelle*—I. [ii.] 145-47]

See the coast cleared, and then we will
   depart.   [*Mayor*—I. [iii.] 102]

Let him that is a true-born gentleman,
And stands upon the honor of his birth,
If he suppose that I have pleaded truth,
From off this brier pluck a white rose with
   me.   [*Plantagenet*—II. [iv.] 31-34]

I'll note you in my book of memory.
                [*Plantagenet*—II. [iv.] 111]

Here dies the dusky torch of Mortimer,
Choked with ambition of the meaner sort.
             [*Plantagenet*—II. [v.] 123-24]

Friendly counsel cuts off many foes.   [*King*—III. i. 201]

Defer no time, delays have dangerous ends.
                 [*Reignier*—III. ii. 34]

Care is no cure, but rather corrosive.   [*Pucelle*—III. iii. 3]

How are we parked and bounded in a pale,
A little herd of England's timorous deer.
                 [*Talbot*—IV. [ii.] 45-6]

She's beautiful and therefore to be wooed;
She is a woman, therefore to be won.
                [*Suffolk*—[V.] iii. 82-4]